HERE COMES THE BEST MAN

When troubled army veteran and musician Josh Robertson returns home to Nashville to be the best man at his younger brother Chad's wedding, he's sure that he's going to mess it all up somehow. But when it becomes clear that the wedding might not be going to plan, it's up to him and fellow guest Louise Giles to save the day. Can Josh be the best man his brother needs? And is there somebody else who is beginning to realise that Josh could be her 'best man' too?

Acknowledgements

We all know writing is a largely solitary endeavour and this is a tribute to all of the people who spend their days with imaginary characters and therefore don't consider me odd, at least no odder than they are! The friendships I've made through my membership of the Music City Romance Writers, Romance Writers of America and Romantic Novelists' Association are invaluable. We are always there for each other to celebrate, encourage and commiserate along the rocky road to publication and beyond.

Thank you also to the Tasting Panel readers who passed this novella and made publication possible: Isobel J, Kim L, Claire W, Karen M, Leanne F, Gina H, Alma H, Ruth N, Jo O, Isabelle D, Sam E, Susan D, LaTonya H, Ester V, Alison G, Catherine L, Dimi E, Thatsany R, Bianca B, Joy S and Jenny M.

1

The things he did for his brother. Josh set his guitar case on the ground, hauled his old army duffle bag up over his shoulder and reached for the brass pineapple-shaped doorknocker. The irony of the traditional symbol of Southern hospitality didn't escape him and he let it fall with a heavy thud.

'Mr Joshua, what on earth are you doin' standing out here on the step? Come in and give me a hug, you naughty boy.' Before he could answer Betty Lou pulled him into her warm embrace. The housekeeper's familiar aroma of baking mixed with lemon furniture polish sur-rounded him and Josh's throat tightened. 'You're early. They told me you wouldn't be here for supper.'

'That's because he thinks he's still Special Ops and prefers the element of surprise. Right, bro?' Chad strode into the hall, grinning from ear to ear.

Trust his smart-ass lawyer brother to nail it in one.

'Why didn't you call? I'd have picked you up at the airport.'

'I drove.' Josh hitched a thumb towards his battered pick-up truck.

'Drove? Heck, how long did that take?'

Josh shrugged. 'Couple of days.'

'But . . . '

'I'm here. All right? I promised I'd be here today and I am.'

Chad slapped his shoulder. 'Yeah and I'm grateful. If you didn't turn up Maggie and I were all set to come and drag you back here by your heels.'

'Where is the lovely lady?' he asked.

'Is that my smooth talking soon-to-be brother-in-law?' Maggie hurried in from the kitchen, hastily rubbing her flour-covered hands on her apron. Her big blue eyes sparkled as they rested on him but Josh noticed a layer of tiredness hanging around her. 'It's lovely to see you again.' She pressed a warm kiss on his cheek and instantly went to Chad's side.

Their unabashed love for each other sent an unwitting flash of envy stabbing through Josh. He'd never forget Chad's unexpected phone call from their cousin Peter's wedding in Cornwall last year for two reasons. The first was his younger brother's out-of-the-blue apology for as he put it, *'being a lousy brother. Not helping when you needed it. Everything I guess'*. The second revolved around Maggie. Chad rhapsodised about the beautiful Englishwoman he'd met which touched Josh to the core and rattled the bones of his own solitary life.

'I hope you're not going to lead this man of mine astray?' Maggie asked.

'Who, me?' Josh teased. He couldn't help having a soft spot for Maggie. Everyone did. The English girl was the warmest, sweetest woman imaginable and his brother was a lucky man. No doubt everyone in Nashville loved her already.

'I'll hold you responsible if I hear

about any strippers at the bachelor party.' Maggie wagged her finger at him.

He threw his brother a horrified glance.

'Don't fret,' Chad murmured, 'you'll be okay.'

I wish I had your confidence.

'I'll warn you now we've got a house full. The English wedding crowd arrived yesterday and Mom's insisted they all stay here.' Chad's smile faltered. 'Our folks are anxious to see you.'

Josh strived to appear unconcerned. He could cope with his mother fussing over him but his father was another story. Their chequered history went all the way back to Josh's childhood and he couldn't remember a time when they'd got on. The prospect of facing Big J Robertson again was one reason he'd taken his sweet time getting here. 'I'm goin' up to drop off my gear then I'll be back down.'

'Don't take too long.' Chad warned and followed Maggie away from the door.

ANGELA BRITNELL

HERE COMES THE BEST MAN

Complete and Unabridged

LINFORD
Leicester

First published in Great Britain in 2018

First Linford Edition
published 2019

A catalogue record for this book is available
from the British Library.

ISBN 978–1–4448–4004–9

Published by
F. A. Thorpe (Publishing)
Anstey, Leicestershire

Set by Words & Graphics Ltd.
Anstey, Leicestershire
Printed and bound in Great Britain by
T. J. International Ltd., Padstow, Cornwall

This book is printed on acid-free paper

Dedication

To Brita and Julie, my two wonderful daughters-in-law. The old saying about losing your sons when they marry was wrong in my case because I discovered if you're fortunate you gain loving daughters without going through the pain of childbirth!

For a few seconds Josh simply focused on breathing, one of the few coping techniques that stuck with him out of the therapy he'd reluctantly attended after his last tour in Afghanistan. With a heavy sigh he made his way up the stairs to his old bedroom.

Talk about time standing still. His high school football trophies still lined the walls and the prized poster of Courtney Love in all her messy hair, leather-jacket, guitar-wielding finest was curling at the edges. The summer he turned fifteen he'd saved up all the money he made cutting lawns to buy the fancy six-CD changer now languishing on top of the bookcase.

Josh caught sight of a dark red leather case propped up in the corner and his heart skipped a beat. He'd purposely left the custom-made acoustic version of the famous Robertson Firebird guitar behind when he left home. Why? In some damn fool effort to stick one to his father who'd proudly given it to him on his sixteenth birthday, signed by

Johnny Cash one of Josh's musical idols. Instead of 'Sing a Song of Sixpence' his mother's lullaby was more likely to be 'Ring of Fire'. While his friends were into Depeche Mode and Madonna he gravitated towards the classic country songs with their stories of love, loss, hope and disappointment.

His family was waiting downstairs but the draw of the music pulled harder. Sitting cross-legged on the narrow twin bed he eased the barely used guitar out of the case, stroking his fingers over the sleek mahogany body built with stunning curves to rival Cindy Crawford in her prime. The shiny red nitro finish screamed rock star, something his father had known would appeal to his rebellious teenage son. Quietly he worked on tuning the beautiful piece back to life before strumming the first few chords of 'Folsom Prison Blues'.

'Hey Josh, you comin' down anytime soon?' Chad pushed open the door and frowned. 'I've caught Dad in here several times over the years looking at that thing. It's soundin' good.'

He quietly stuck the guitar back in the case. 'Let's go.'

* * *

Louise came close to choking on an ice cube when she met the stranger's dark, flinty gaze. The man fixed his attention on her for several impolite seconds before turning away.

'That must be Chandler's brother,' Audrey murmured and Louise turned her attention back to her employer. 'From what I've heard he's a difficult man and rather the black sheep of the family. I'd stay away if you know what's good for you.' People frequently took Audrey Trembarth's forthright manner the wrong way but after five years living with her in Cornwall and working as her personal assistant Louise wasn't at all offended. Like many Englishwomen of her generation and upbringing Audrey had a low tolerance for fools and no patience with the modern habit for people baring their souls to all and sundry. The fact Louise was thirty-five years old compared to Audrey's seventy-five meant little and the two women understood each other well.

'You don't need to worry.' Louise wasn't naive and had learned her lessons about men the hard way. Her unequivocal reply gained her an approving nod from Audrey.

'Audrey, this is my older brother, Josh.' Chad suddenly appeared and with one flash of his charming smile made the older woman blush like a teenage girl.

Louise knew her employer had been initially wary of the American but had learned to accept his deep love for her god-daughter, a girl she valued deeply. Audrey and Chad's unconventional friend-ship developed further through their mutual passion for all things Art Deco, bringing a new sparkle to her life. When Maggie announced her intention to be married in Nashville the long distance and her less than perfect health were never going to stop Audrey from attending.

'Josh, this is Maggie's godmother and honorary great-aunt, Audrey Trembarth. She'll give the impression she's a dragon but really she's a pussy cat.'

Louise suppressed a smile. No one else would dare speak to her that way.

'She owns the absolute coolest Art Deco house in Cornwall plus an amazing ceramics collection. Dad would willingly give his right arm for her Clarice Cliff pottery.'

'Sit down, young man, and tell me about yourself.' Audrey shooed Chad away. 'This is Louise Giles, my personal assistant.'

'Pleased to meet you, ma'am.'

Louise stuck out her hand and for a heartbeat he simply stared before taking it in a firm clasp and sending a bolt of heat through her blood. The superficial resemblance to his younger brother ended at his mesmerising tawny eyes and thick jet-black hair. There was no smooth charming veneer to Josh Robertson, only a dark, hard world-weariness he wore like a heavy winter coat.

'I understand you live in Colorado?' Audrey interrupted and Louise took the opportunity to retrieve her hand.

'Yes, ma'am.'

'You served in the army for several years?'

'Yes, ma'am.'

Audrey frowned. 'Do you know any other words apart from 'yes, ma'am'? Your brother is a very intelligent conversationalist.'

'I sure do, ma'am, but I'm not Chad.'

'We're all different thank goodness. I hope you have your speech prepared for the wedding and won't let them down.'

A brooding shadow flitted across Josh's face and Louise experienced a surge of pity for him. The big, brawny man with his worn jeans and heavy work boots appeared out of place in his own family home. She understood all about being out of place. Despite an unstable childhood and fractured education she'd fought hard to rise above it and make a stable life for herself. At the back of her mind there still remained a lingering fear that it could all disappear in a puff of smoke.

'I'll sure try not to, ma'am,' he muttered. Josh rubbed one large hand absently over his dark stubbly jaw line. 'I'd better make the rounds and meet everyone else.' His grim tone implied he'd rather stand in front of a firing squad.

'I'm sure none of them will bite,' Louise whispered, unduly pleased when the faint hint of a smile tugged at his stern mouth. 'We were well fed at lunch.'

'That's good news, ma'am.' The touch of amusement spread to his eyes, brightening the tawny flecks to golden sparks of light.

'Please don't keep calling me that, it makes me sound ancient.'

Josh nodded. 'Sure thing, Louise.' His smooth, deep drawl trickled over her and Louise's heart thudded against her chest. He stood up, gave a polite nod to them both and strode away.

'Oh dear you're going to ignore my advice, aren't you?' Audrey shook her head.

'Whatever do you — '

'Maggie and the bad-mannered American she's marrying were exactly the same.' Louise didn't argue over her employer's description of Chad because she knew Audrey didn't mean a word of it. 'I saw their interest in each other at Fiona's wedding reception and they refused to listen to my warning.'

Louise bit her lip. She'd give anything to be as happy as the pair standing in front of the ornate marble fireplace and gazing into each others' eyes as though the world started and ended right there. Everyone knew the fascinating story of Chad arriving at his English cousin's wedding only to be bewitched by Maggie, the lonely cake decorator. But Audrey was wrong this time.

Louise hadn't worked hard in order to toss it away for any man. One man almost derailed her but she'd mostly managed to put the disaster with Craig Merton behind her now and determined never to be that foolish and naive again.

'I hope you prove me wrong, my dear.' Audrey gave a wry smile. 'We both know that's something I rarely say.'

'Would you care for another cup of tea?' Louise deliberately changed the subject.

'Remember to — '

'Go to the kitchen and make it myself properly.' Other people considered Audrey to be inflexible but Louise appreciated knowing where she stood and what was expected of her. 'I won't be long,' she promised. Out in the empty hall she stood still for a moment and allowed the buzz of conversation to fade into the background. *Sure thing, Louise.* Josh's words reverberated in her head and she gave herself a mental shake.

2

'How about we go get you a few new things to wear tomorrow, Josh?'

'I've got plenty of clothes, Mom.' He tried to think of something to say to placate her. 'How about you show me the garden? Should be looking good this time of year.'

'The garden? Now?' Tricia glanced around the crowded room and an anxious furrow creased the space between her brows.

'I could do with a touch of fresh air.'

'I suppose we can. Let me go and fetch your dad.'

'No.' He'd so far avoided anything beyond a quick handshake and an in-depth conversation with Big J wasn't on his agenda. 'I want to catch up on how you're doin'.' Before she could protest he steered her towards the French doors. 'Y'all are happy about the wedding?' The second they stepped out into the late afternoon sunshine the warmth seeped into his bones and he started to relax.

'Absolutely. Maggie's a complete sweetheart. I must admit I fretted some before Chad brought her here the first time but she's fitted right on in and sure does love your brother.' She hesitated. 'Have you found yourself a nice girl out there in Colorado?'

'Not yet, Mom.' Josh didn't think a brief chat once a month with the supermarket cashier counted, especially as the lady in question was at least sixty and comfortably married with a huge brood of children and grandchildren. A brief image of Louise Giles' smoky grey eyes and enigmatic smile sneaked in but he blinked it away.

'Chad's settling into the business real good. Your father's pleased with him.'

But not with me. I get it. 'That's great.'

Tricia flushed. 'I didn't mean — '

'Hey, it's all right, Mom. I couldn't

do it.' He cleared his throat, fighting against the sudden tightness. 'Dad needs the help. I understand. It's okay.' Traditionally the eldest Robertson son took over running the venerable guitar company started by his great-grandfather but Josh bucked the trend. For a host of reasons he'd refused to have anything to do with the business and defied his father by joining the army at eighteen. Big J would never forgive him.

'Are you staying busy?'

'Yeah. I take care of my land and I've started to escort a few guided hikes around the area for a local tour operator.' Josh wished he could tell her he'd found the sort of steady job she'd approve of but he wouldn't lie.

'That sure is good to hear.'

His mother's forced smile pained him. Josh ached to explain that the move to Colorado a year before had saved him from falling into the same black hole as so many other veterans, but if he tried she'd ask too many questions he wasn't prepared to answer.

He'd seen plenty of his fellow soldiers, decent men and women who'd given so much and served their country, stumble and fall over trying to fit back into civilian life. Josh had struggled too at first, rootless and aimless. With no fixed purpose and no need to earn a living immediately he'd sunk into a dangerous spiral. Too stubborn to move back home he woke up in his rented hotel room with another throbbing hangover and focused his bleary eyes on the family photograph on his bedside table, feeling their shame seeping into him. He took a temporary job with a local landscaping company and the long hours of hard physical labour started his turnaround. The morning he'd overheard a couple of his co-workers argue about who'd drunk the last bottle of water from the office fridge he'd quit. They'd made it seem like a matter of life and death and Josh came close to grabbing the men by the throat and yelling that they didn't have a goddamn clue. That's when he spelled it out to his folks that joining the business wasn't an option and fled to save his own sanity.

'You're looking better these days.'

He didn't call her out on the obvious lie. At least she hadn't added the traditional 'bless your heart' — a common southern expression used to express disapproval under a layer of sympathy. Even Goodwill wouldn't accept Josh's old clothes, his last haircut was six months ago and his haphazard shave could serve as the before picture for a razor commercial.

'I'll clean up for the wedding,' he promised.

'I know you won't let Maggie and Chad down, sweetheart.'

'But?' Josh challenged but she didn't answer and reached out to pinch off a dead leaf from the nearest bush. 'You're worried about all of Maggie's family in there and what they'll think.' His mother turned back around and her soft blue eyes glimmered with unshed tears. 'Hey, don't get upset. They'll be off back home to England next week.'

'Mom, the florist is here and Maggie needs your help.' Chad sauntered out to join them. 'Sorry to interrupt, bro.'

Josh would've hugged his brother if they did touchy-feely stuff, which they didn't. 'No problem. She's all yours.' He let them go, gathering the strength to go back inside and do his duty. He didn't break promises and Chad had pleaded with him to be in Nashville for the week leading up to the wedding.

I need you by my side. You're my big brother and you owe me.

Chad was right. At eighteen Josh enlisted in the army and gave little thought to the eight-year-old brother he left behind to bear the weight of their parents' expectations. When his time came Chad dug in his heels too and refused to join the family business out of stubbornness, despite loving everything about Robertson guitars, and went into entertainment law. It took Maggie's steady loving influence to make him see sense and now Chad worked alongside their father and couldn't be happier.

Josh exhaled a heavy sigh and trudged back towards the house.

★　★　★

'Are you sure there's nothing else you need?' Louise asked, checking she'd left a glass of water and Audrey's favourite peppermints within reach on the bedside table.

'Stop fussing.'

'I'm sorry.'

'Go and have a good walk, girl, for heaven's sake. I don't have one foot in the grave quite yet. I'll see you in the morning.'

'Thank you.' She hurried into the adjoining bedroom and kicked off her shoes before unzipping the pale grey dress and wriggling out of it with relief. Louise hung the dress up carefully and replaced it with a pair of tan shorts and an old blue T-shirt. Tennessee in early May was delightful, warm enough to be enjoyable but without the searing summer heat. She made her way downstairs and stopped to speak to Chad's mother in the hall. Soon she'd been given instructions as to where to go and was shooed out of the back door with the order to enjoy herself.

She'd heard the discussion earlier about whether to go to the Nashville Zoo tomorrow or have a tour of the city. She might be wrong but Josh's awkwardness around them all made her suspect he wouldn't care for either option. *Stop thinking about the man. Remember what you promised Audrey. And yourself.*

Louise set off at a steady pace along the walking trail that ran parallel to the back of Magnolia House. The pre-Civil War mansion with its ornate columns, sweeping porch and original antique furniture was incredible. Being such a huge contrast to Holland House, Audrey's Art Deco era home overlooking St. Ives Bay, made it even more interesting. The Robertson estate had apparently been far more extensive but the family donated a large portion of the land to the city to be turned into a public park.

'Hey, slow down, or are you being chased by wolves?'

She jerked to a halt at the sound of Josh's deep voice. 'Oh, it's you. Why are you sneaking up on me?'

'I wasn't . . . ' Josh's granite features softened. 'Sorry. I guess I did. Force of habit.' A devilish smile crept across his face, taking years off of him.

'Do you mind if I keep walking?'

'Do you mind if I join you?' Josh laughingly mimicked her words.

'It's Robertson land. Feel free.'

★   ★   ★

Josh let her stride ahead. He could easily catch up with her if he chose but the view was too good from where he stood. Snug fitting shorts. Long shapely legs. *And don't forget the T-shirt cling-ing to some grade-A curves.* Definitely a huge improvement on the dreary grey

22

dress. He smiled to himself. Chad often joked about the ugly green dress Maggie was wearing the day they met. She'd apparently worn it to ten years' worth of weddings until his brother threatened to chop it into tiny pieces if he ever saw it again.

'You're slow.'

She'd taken a seat on the bench and waited for him. *Interesting.* Josh joined her, stretched out his legs and rested his hands behind his head. 'How long have you worked for the Dragon Lady?'

'She's not a . . . ' A smile curved her generous, unpainted lips. 'You're teasing me.'

'Never.'

'I've been with Mrs Trembarth about five years.'

'Where did you work before that?' Josh noticed her faltering smile and guessed he'd hit on a sore subject.

'I had various jobs in the art world which is how I came to meet Audrey.' She stood back up. 'This isn't getting me much in the way of exercise. If you'll excuse me.'

'I guess I'll sit here a while longer.' Josh waited to see if she'd encourage him to join her but Louise simply nodded. He tried to be grateful but did a lousy job of it. Her private business was officially nothing to do with him but she still intrigued him. Chad had made him promise to be friendly to the English wedding guests so he'd start with Audrey. The old lady liked to talk. He needed a few answers. It should be a perfect combination.

3

Louise crept downstairs and tried her best not to disturb the rest of the house. Audrey expected her early morning cup of tea at precisely seven o'clock and if she didn't hurry now it'd be late. She inched open the kitchen door then froze in place at the sound of Chad's pleading voice.

'I'm sorry, sweetheart. I know this means a lot to you.'

'But it shouldn't. They're only flowers. I'm turning into one of *them*!' Maggie wailed and burst into loud wracking sobs.

Louise couldn't back out of the kitchen fast enough before the couple spotted her. 'Sorry. I didn't know anyone else was up yet.'

Maggie wriggled out of her fiancé's arms and wiped ineffectually at her red-rimmed eyes. 'Come in. I've boiled the kettle. Maybe a cup of tea will help.'

'Are you sure you want company?'

'Yes. We were talking, or I should say arguing, about the flowers.'

She wasn't sure how to respond. Last night Audrey commented how much thinner and more tired her goddaughter looked and Louise had tried to assure her that every bride lost weight and worried but what did she know? Weddings weren't her thing. On the remote chance she ever got married it would be a ten-minute ceremony at a register office. After all she had no family who'd be interested in attending and wasn't going to waste her hard earned money on things like a wickedly expensive dress she'd only wear for a couple of hours. There'd be no southern mansion and a guest list that included the cream of Nashville's country music royalty for her.

'Maggie is disappointed because the florist brought some samples over and the orchids are the Ming yellow of a Chinese silk robe as opposed to a Dahlia yellow which apparently resembles sun-drenched Italy.' Chad's dry recitation implied he'd had these differences drummed into him and still didn't get it.

'I know it's dumb.' Maggie's sad tone tugged at Louise's heart. 'I've worked with so many brides over the years and even dragged my pregnant sister unscathed through her wedding.' The taut smile she attempted didn't reach her deep blue eyes. 'You would think I'd know better.'

'She's convinced she's turning into a Bridezilla.' Chad slipped an arm around his bride-to-be. 'I told her we'll get through this but she doesn't believe me.'

'I want to.' Maggie's anguish was palpable.

'But I thought everything was organised. Doesn't everyone here use a wedding planner?' Louise chose her words carefully because she sensed it wouldn't take much to set her poor friend off again.

'I pictured something small and intimate and convinced Chad's mother we could easily pull it together our-selves, but . . . ' Maggie stumbled over her explanation and a hot blush lit up her fair, freckled skin. 'They don't understand me, Louise. They're too busy oohing and aahing over my accent and saying how cute I am. I did a lot of the planning long distance before we arrived but my ideas seem to have got lost in translation.' She shrugged apologetically at Chad. 'I love your mother but our styles are vastly different. I'm too polite to speak up so instead I get mad and seethe. Anyway it's far too late to change anything with only six days left.'

'It doesn't help that my hardworking fiancée is trying to get her wedding cake business re-established here at the same time and she's taken on too many jobs with a tight deadline. She's run ragged.' Chad shook his head with frustration.

'Do you want me to help?' Louise blurted out and Maggie and Chad stared at her in disbelief. 'I can't offer to do any baking but I could take some of the burden off as far as the actual wedding is concerned. I'm good at organising and I know how to stand up for myself.' She smiled. 'Audrey's made sure of that.'

'Are you serious?' Chad asked. 'Audrey won't stand for being neglected.'

Louise scoffed. 'She'd be thrilled because she'll expect to stick her oar in and interfere — which I won't allow. I can't promise a miracle but if I can deal with the last minute details you could take a step back.'

'Naturally we'd compensate you well for your time,' Chad assured her.

'Oh please don't say that. It would be my gift to you both.'

'We couldn't possibly — '

Maggie cut him off. 'Thanks, Louise. It's a very kind offer and we'd love to accept.'

'Yeah, we would,' Chad parroted and his wide grin lit up the room. 'I've gotta get in practise for being an obedient husband.'

'I'm sure you'll get it right after about fifty years,' Louise joked.

'I sure hope so.'

'Gosh. I feel so much better already,' Maggie announced. 'I'm going to cook breakfast and maybe I'll actually manage to eat something for a change. If it makes my wedding dress too tight I really don't care. I'm afraid I don't like it much anyway,' she whispered. 'I only chose it to stop Chad's sweet mother trailing me around more shops.'

'I need to take a tray of tea up to Audrey. I'll get something to eat myself later,' Louise explained. 'As soon you've got some spare time today we'll sit down and talk. I need every detail of what's already been planned and what you'd like changed — but remember I'm not making any promises.' They stared as though she'd grown a second head. 'Is something wrong?'

'Nope. I think we've unleashed the right person on this whole mess,' Chad declared with a warm chuckle.

What had she let herself in for?

★ ★ ★

Josh stopped in the empty kitchen to fix himself a mug of coffee before he strolled out into the hall. He checked the family room and didn't find anybody around. *There was his quarry.* Josh spotted Audrey sitting on her own in the screened-in porch reading the newspaper.

He'd treated this as another mission and done his preparations before coming downstairs. The dark slacks and slightly crumpled white shirt were the best he owned and he'd taken care to slick down his hair and give himself a proper close shave. He'd even sneaked into Chad's room and borrowed a pair of black leather shoes after recalling Audrey's disparaging grimace when she'd spotted his dirty work boots the previous evening.

'Good morning, ma'am. Do you mind if I join you?'

Her shrewd gaze swept over him and Josh stood his ground, returning her eagle-eyed stare straight on.

'Sit down. It is your house, despite

the fact you behave as though it isn't. Can you believe they asked me to go to the zoo with them today?' Audrey held up a warning hand before he could respond. 'And don't even think of suggesting they might have planned to leave me there.'

'Chad hit the nail on the head, you sure are something else.' He chuckled.

'Is this for my benefit?' She gestured at his clothes. 'And if so, why?'

The old Chad used to claim the reason Josh failed with women was because of his habit of being completely honest. That was in his pre-Maggie days but she'd seen right through Chad and demanded he change his ways. 'Don't mind admitting I tidied up partly for you because I wanna pick your brains.'

Audrey's eyebrows raised but she didn't speak.

Josh took a swig of his coffee and wondered how best to approach the question.

'If you're going to ask me about

Louise you're wasting your time.'

His face burned. *Was he so transparent?*

'Whatever she chooses to tell you or not is her business. You're not getting any gossip out of me.' Audrey picked up the newspaper again, glancing at him over the top of her glasses as if to say 'are you still here?'

'Did she go to the zoo?'

'You are persistent.' He picked up the first hint of approval and suppressed a smile. 'Yes she did go but when they return this afternoon she'll be busy. We've all noticed how strained Maggie is looking and this morning Louise offered to help with the wedding plans and take some of the burden off my poor goddaughter.'

'I noticed she wasn't her usual bright self but I assumed it was a bride thing.'

'Nonsense. All brides diet and worry, it comes with the territory but Maggie is miserable. She plasters a smile back on when it's needed because she's a trooper.'

His head spun. 'Are you saying she doesn't want to marry Chad?'

'Don't be ridiculous. Do you possess a brain under all that hair?'

The Brits should use Audrey as a lethal weapon. She'd be much cheaper than any atomic bomb and far more deadly.

'Maggie's main fault is the fact she's too nice. She apparently agreed to make two wedding cakes for new customers before next weekend but doesn't really have the time. Maggie still needs to finish her own cake along with seeing to all the last minute wedding details. She's gone along with everything your mother suggested and it's not working. Louise will try to put some of that right,' Audrey declared with an air of satisfaction.

'Isn't it too late? The wedding's on Saturday.'

'It's never too late. Remember that.'

He got the distinct impression they weren't talking about the wedding any longer. No doubt Audrey had spoken to his parents, especially his father. If that was the case *she* was the one barking up the wrong tree. 'Maybe.'

'You could help by taking some of the burden off your brother. He's trying to keep everyone happy and failing miserably.'

Josh shifted in the chair. Audrey didn't know what she was asking. He didn't do crowds. Or parties. Or dressing smartly. These days the list went on and on. In Colorado he'd managed to acquire a relatively healthy balance inside his head and worried about putting that at risk. 'I'll think about it.'

'Don't take too long.'

He got to his feet and headed towards the door.

'Despite what you might think I'm not heartless.' Audrey stopped him in his tracks. 'I know you haven't had an easy time but neither have a lot of people. We all have our sorrows and regrets. We learn to live with them.'

Josh almost asked the older woman

about hers but wasn't that brave. 'I guess I haven't learned how yet but I'm workin' on it.'

'Look at this as an opportunity.'

He managed a tight smile. 'You don't cut people any slack, do you?'

'Were you easy on the men you commanded in the army?'

'Never.' The urge to smile wouldn't go away. 'They called me BB. For Big Bas — '

Audrey held up a hand. 'That's quite enough.'

'Sorry, ma'am. Afraid I forget my manners sometimes.'

'Off with you and leave me alone. I've got things to consider.'

So do I.

4

Louise kept her attention fixed on her laptop and refused to turn around. Every traitorous cell in her body stood to attention when Josh was in the vicinity and right now they were dancing a jig.

'How's your day goin'?' He draped himself over the kitchen counter and rested his elbows on the papers she'd spread out to one side.

'Fine, thank you.' Louise stared at the spreadsheet she'd created and struggled to ignore his rich, warm laugh.

'I had a long chat with your boss this morning.' Josh selected an apple from the bowl and juggled it between his large hands. 'Interesting woman.'

Louise sighed. 'Is there a point to this conversation?' She sneaked a quick glance over at him. Clean shaven. Thick black hair freshly washed and gleaming. Josh smelled deliciously of simple soap and water. Nothing like the last man she'd been attracted to but see how that turned out . . .

Josh took a large bite of the apple and munched his way through the whole thing all the way to the core. 'Yeah. There sure is. I suspect you and me are gonna have to work together.'

'Excuse me?' She listened in dismay as he recited the conversation he'd had with Audrey. Louise found it hard to wrap her head around the idea that her employer had suggested a bizarre collaboration on Maggie and Chad's wedding problems. Considering she'd warned Louise off getting involved with Josh in the first place it made no sense.

'I thought she was crazy at first too but I'm comin' around to the idea.'

'Well I'm not.' Louise shook her head.

'I owe Chad bigtime for a whole lot of reasons. Mainly because he's my only brother and I've let him down enough over the years. Plus Maggie's a sweetheart and deserves the best damn wedding ever.' He absentmindedly rested one large hand over hers making her aware of the warmth and strength under his work-roughened skin. 'Audrey warned me off getting any ideas about you while she was at it.'

'Ideas?' she croaked.

'Yeah, ideas.' Josh's fingers idly stroked over her hand and shards of heat zapped through her blood. 'Of course just because I spent twenty years in the army doesn't mean I always obey orders.'

'In this case it might be wise.'

He scoffed. 'Ask my father. He'd never use that word to describe me.'

Louise tugged her hand away. 'The wedding. Do you want to hear my ideas?' Her abrupt change of topic deepened his smile. Josh pulled out a stool and hitched himself up, reaching for another apple.

'Go ahead.'

'Do you have an apple fetish?'

'I'm fond of apples. You got a

problem with that? It's a harmless addiction — unless you're an apple of course.' He deadpanned. 'Have to say you sure don't look like one to me.'

A rush of embarrassment flamed her cheeks. 'We are totally getting off the point here.'

★   ★   ★

'Go ahead. Get us back on track.' Josh bit down on the apple. He'd been shocked when his rusty flirtation skills seemed to have worked. He might not be a genius when it came to women but even Josh couldn't miss the flare of interest in Louise's eyes.

'I talked to the happy couple when we got back from the zoo and I've drawn up some ideas. The first priority is Maggie's wedding dress. I know fashion isn't your field so I'll take that in hand.'

'Call me dumb — and women usually do — but don't these things take months to arrange?'

Louise snorted. 'Surely you've heard

the saying 'money talks'? Working for Audrey I see it all the time with art experts outbidding each other to garner another piece for their collection. Haven't you experienced the same thing with your family?'

'I guess so.' He wasn't stepping anywhere near that minefield.

'The main problem is that your mother talked Maggie into a meringue and she hates it.'

'I totally get that I'm a clueless man but what am I missing here?' Josh frowned. 'I know Maggie's a cake maker but tell me she's not planning to make a dress out of meringues? Even Southern women aren't *that* crazy.' A wide grin lit up Louise's face and Josh fought to catch his breath as her flash of joy tugged at his heart. He immediately wanted to crack more jokes and chip away at her seemingly serious shell.

'Oh, Josh.' Her crisp English accent softened and something inside him melted. 'A meringue is a style of dress — all sort of poufy and fussy — think

Cinderella at the ball.'

'Yep. Got it now.' He smacked the side of his head with his hand. 'I'll let you into a little secret. I'm a secret expert on all of Cinderella's fashions but I've always hated that one.' He struggled to keep a serious face because he knew it'd make her laugh. *Bingo.*

'You're hopeless.' She giggled. 'It's very un-Maggie and won't suit her at all.'

'Hey, I'll take your word for it. You deal with the dress. What's the next problem?'

'The pre-wedding events start to escalate tomorrow and Maggie will completely lose it if she has to get through all of them.' Louise waved a sheet of paper in his face. 'She's got two wedding cakes to make for clients plus her own to finish before next Saturday. She doesn't have the time for all the lunches, showers and teas.'

'That could be tricky. Get my mom on board with this. If she can drop hints about Maggie being overwhelmed I'm guessing some can be cut out. You could make people feel better by promising to reschedule after the wedding.' He grinned. 'Next?'

'The food for the reception. I'm sure it'll be wonderful but they're all Southern delicacies. Maggie doesn't *dislike* any of it but nothing reflects her English heritage.'

'Isn't that kind of obvious?' Josh laughed at Louise's blank stare. 'Humour me. How did Maggie and Chad meet?'

She sighed with the despairing air of a smart woman faced with a terminally stupid man. 'At the Cornish wedding of your cousin Peter to Maggie's friend, Fiona.'

'Very good. Ten points. Apart from the fact Fiona is her oldest friend why was Maggie there? Ever heard of Two Hearts Catering?'

'It's . . . oh, stupid me.' Louise winced. 'Could I be any denser?'

Only if you fall for me.

'But poor Maggie hasn't got time to cook on top of everything else,' she protested.

'I'm not suggesting she does but weren't the two sisters in business together?' He quickly kept going. 'Maggie was the cake genius and Emily did the regular catering. Maybe if Emily's husband — Jonathan isn't it? — looks after their baby then she can bake whatever Maggie fancies.' He basked in the warmth of Louise's smile.

Her eyes sparkled. 'I'm starting to get more ideas for ramping up the British/American theme. I'll work on that.'

'How are we doin' on your list?' Josh slid off the stool and shifted around to stand behind Louise to better see the laptop screen. A drift of musky perfume teased his nostrils reminding him of rye whisky and long winter nights in front of a crackling fire. An unusual choice for the cool, calm facade Louise presented to the world but it suited the woman he saw underneath. Josh cleared his throat, fighting down a sudden overwhelming desire to kiss her.

'The list.'

The husky edge to her voice encouraged him to brush aside a lock of silky ash-blonde hair that'd escaped its tight knot and stroke a finger along her pale, smooth skin. 'Yeah, the list.'

'Don't.' Her breathy plea touched him. 'Please.'

Regret laced through her words and lingered in her smoky grey eyes. Josh drew on every last reserve of patience and dropped his hands back down to his side. 'I'll apologise if you want me to.'

'Maybe *I* should?'

'Why? For being beautiful, witty and intelligent? For arousing my interest?' Josh shook his head. 'Bad timing. That's all. One of my many faults.' He dismissed his awkward seduction attempt with a shrug. 'I'll run the idea by Emily and Jonathan and touch base with you later.' He hurried away and closed the kitchen door firmly on the way out. If it wasn't for letting down Chad he'd get in his truck and hightail it back to Colorado.

5

Louise had compartmentalising down to a fine art and forced herself to lock away the image of Josh's granite features changing into a heart-stopping smile and tying her in knots. She started by making an appointment to meet Maggie's wedding dress designer in the morning before setting off to track down Chad's mother.

'Hello, Mrs Robertson.' Her cheery greeting made the other woman look up from her wedding planning book, a two inch thick white leather bible she'd bragged about starting the day Maggie and Chad got engaged.

'Call me Tricia, hon we don't stand on ceremony around here.'

'Thanks. Do you mind if I join you?'

'Sit down.' Tricia patted the seat next to her on the sofa. 'What've you been up to since we got back from the zoo?

Audrey's a tad on the scary side, isn't she?'

'She can appear that way but she's really a very kind woman underneath.' Louise stopped herself from saying too much. 'This might sound an odd question but are you at all worried about the wedding?'

'Apart from the gazillion details to sort out before next Saturday?' Tricia laughed. 'No. Why?'

'Good evening, ladies.' Mr Robertson strode into the room and his striking resemblance to Josh rattled her. Both sons had inherited their dark good looks from their father rather than their petite, blonde mother. 'Are you both staying out of mischief?'

'Louise was asking if we're worried about the wedding but I'm not sure what she's getting at.'

His warm smile faded and the abrupt change unsettled Louise.

'Why are you askin'?'

Louise took a deep breath and plunged in. By the time she finished telling them about her conversation with Maggie and Chad the temperature in the room had plummeted to sub-zero.

'It's too damn late now,' Mr Robertson declared. 'They'll have to suck it up. This time next week it'll all be over and they'll be on honeymoon. A luxury resort on a private Caribbean island. Not much of a hardship.'

'But I hate to think Maggie's unhappy, dear. Or Chad. I didn't mean to bully them.' Tricia's eyes welled with tears.

'Oh, but you didn't.' Louise hurried to reassure her. 'Maggie appreciates everything you've done but she's simply been too nice to speak up and give her honest opinion. Chad didn't interfere because she begged him not to. She's aware she shouldn't have taken on the other wedding cake commissions but has to see them through now.'

Mr Robertson's brow furrowed. The nickname Big J suited him and not only because of his large physique. This was a man used to getting his own way.

'If you want to fiddle about with the dresses and the food go ahead.' He held up a warning finger. 'But the parties aren't negotiable. We're not gonna let down our family and friends.'

She felt irrationally upset at his refusal and then jerked her head around as Josh burst into the room.

★   ★   ★

'Still pushing people around, Dad?' Josh had overheard enough through the half-open door. 'Louise is only trying to help.'

'Watch your tongue, son.'

'Sorry but you're only seeing things from your point of view — as usual.'

'Oh Josh, dear, please calm down.' His mother stepped in to referee, something she'd done all his life.

'No. Let the boy say what's been bugging him ever since he set foot back in this house.' Big J's booming voice ricocheted around the room but Josh stood his ground and didn't flinch.

'What on earth's going on?' Chad ran in, glaring around at everyone. 'You've woken the baby with all your shouting and Emily just got poor little Rose off to sleep.'

'Sorry, bro.' Josh apologised before Louise could do the same. He wouldn't allow her to take the blame. 'We're trying to sort out a few of the hang-ups with the wedding plans, that's all.'

'Oh, right. Anything you can do to make my lady happy gets my vote. Make me wear an Elvis impersonator suit and serve boiled okra for all I care if it'll cheer up Maggie. I don't give a damn about anything as long as we end up married.'

No wonder his brother was such a great lawyer. Chad could defuse any situation with his charming smile, making Josh wish he'd inherited some of their mother's easy manner. 'The jury is still out on the Elvis suit but the okra's a definite.' He dredged up a tight smile.

'I wish y'all could encourage Maggie to eat more.' Chad's voice faltered. 'I'm not goin' to have anything left to grab a hold of at this rate.'

'She'll be okay. This time next week it'll all be over.' Josh repeated back his father's words and caught Big J raise one thick dark eyebrow behind his brother's back. 'Go back upstairs and fuss over your bride-to-be. We'll sort this out.' He'd do this for Chad even if it took tying up his father until after the wedding.

Once Chad left the room Josh turned back to face them all. 'Are we in this together?'

'I'm in.' Louise instantly backed him up and he could've kissed her. *Yeah, well, you want to do that every time you see the woman so that's not news.*

'And me. All I want is a happy day they'll remember forever,' Tricia declared with a steely edge to her voice.

'Fine,' Big J muttered. 'Don't think we're done, boy.' He threw Josh another fierce stare. 'When this is over you and me are talkin'.' He stalked out of the room and Josh's mother flashed an apologetic smile before running after him.

'Goodness.' Louise fanned herself with the wedding to-do list she'd been holding on to. 'Is life in your house always this — '

'Dramatic?' Josh shrugged. 'Only when I'm around.' Her silence told him she was waiting for more. 'Dad and I tended to butt heads when I was growing up. He had my path mapped out before I was born the same as it'd been for him with his father. I'd follow him into the family business and eventually take over Robertson Guitars. But that wasn't what I wanted. It's one of the reasons I joined the army.'

'And the others?'

'Nothing you'd be interested in. Hey, how about a drink? We deserve one after all that.' Her sympathetic smile told Josh she'd picked up on his sad attempt to divert the conversation.

'I'd really love to but Audrey will

wonder where I am.'

She stood up and Josh caught another hint of her sultry perfume. Louise's clear grey eyes darkened as they rested on him and he ached to touch her. Heavy footsteps thundered upstairs and a streak of commonsense penetrated Josh's brain. 'You'd better run off and reassure Audrey I haven't abducted you. I'm gonna have that drink.'

'Good night, Josh. I've got a lot to do tomorrow. Shall we meet for a progress report before dinner? Say around five?'

'That's a date.' He quickly waved one hand around in the air. 'This is me with an imaginary white flag. I didn't mean that the way it came out.'

'Didn't you?'

For a second Josh almost blurted out the truth but the wobble in her voice stopped him.

'Leave it. Okay?'

'Will do.' Josh grunted and walked over to the cocktail cabinet, before changing his mind and walking away.

He didn't have any problem with taking an occasional drink these days but there'd been a song buzzing around his head for hours trying to get out. Instead of his father's best twelve-year-old single malt whiskey he'd hole up in his room and discover what his Robertson Firebird could really do.

6

Louise felt a distinct sense of accomplishment. With Tricia's help they'd postponed two bridal teas, one luncheon and two cocktail parties and replaced them with a post-honeymoon 'special' party for 'honoured' guests. She'd also talked the designer into donating Maggie's extravagant wedding dress to a military bride-to-be. Louise walked a fine line trying to express Maggie's unhappiness with the dress without offending the designer's sensibilities. She'd used the 'what great publicity it will garner' card and freed herself to search elsewhere. With only six days to go. No pressure.

So far she'd avoided Josh, only catching a flash of his dark hair as he disappeared out of the front door after breakfast.

'Tell my crazy sister to stay out of the

kitchen or I'm going to kill her.' Emily burst into the room followed by a red-faced Maggie shouting something unintelligible.

'Why don't you both sit down and we'll have a quiet chat.' Louise quickly intervened before things turned nasty. 'The last thing we want is to wake up Emily's sweet baby. What's the problem?'

'She's the problem.' Emily tossed a fierce glare at her sister. 'Miss Know-it-all won't let me get on with my cooking. I'm the caterer not her. I don't stick my nose in when she's fiddling about with her fancy cakes. You wouldn't think I'm doing her a favour,' she complained. 'I'm supposed to be enjoying a nice holiday with my husband not making hundreds of sausage rolls and mini-quiches.'

'If that's how you feel I don't want your stupid food,' Maggie screeched, wiping furiously at the tears dripping down her face. 'Damn it all. I never cry. What the hell's wrong with me?'

Emily smirked. 'You're being a bride instead of my super-efficient responsible sister for once.' She slipped her arm around Maggie's shoulder. 'Welcome to the world of normal people.'

'I'm sorry. We never meant to force you into anything,' Louise apologised.

'You didn't. I want to help. She knows that really.'

Maggie smiled through her gulping sobs and hugged her sister. 'Are we okay now?'

'Of course. You've always been there for me even when I was a pain in the you-know-what,' Emily joked. 'It's my turn now.'

'You were *always* a pain.' Maggie rolled her eyes. 'I'm simply grateful I got you married off and now you're Jonathan's problem.'

'Yes, well, in a few days I can palm *you* off on poor defenceless Chad.'

Louise's throat tightened. Despite their bickering these two would never let each other down but she knew things hadn't always been this way between them. Audrey confided in her once that as a child Maggie was forced to take a back seat to her emotionally volatile sister and the situation got worse when Emily blamed Maggie for their mother's accidental death. Chad became their guardian angel when he encouraged the two sisters to let go of their old misconceptions about each other. Now Louise had discovered a little more of his story she was sure he'd drawn on his own estrangement from Josh and worked to put that right too.

Seeing the two women now gave Louise a sliver of hope for her broken relationship with her own half-sister. Poor Jules had done her very best and Louise threw it right back in her face. Having a rebellious fourteen-year-old dumped on her because their mother couldn't cope any longer must have been hard. Louise had disrupted Jules' family, taking time and attention away from her husband and small children. She'd skipped school on a regular basis and run away so often Jules became on first name terms with the local police. The last time she ran off was the day after her sixteenth birthday and no one came searching for her. Louise came to the conclusion her sister had justifiably washed her hands of her. She'd never felt so alone but her stubborn teenage pride hadn't allowed her to return and plead for another chance. Perhaps she'd find the courage soon to make the first move and apologise. There was no guarantee Jules would be willing to forgive her but it had to be worth a try.

'Emily, why don't you get back to the kitchen and knock out a hundred more sausage rolls?' She tried to lighten the moment. 'Maggie and I need to discuss her dress.'

'Oh God, must we?' Maggie groaned. 'There's nothing you can do. I'm going to roll down the aisle in that ugly frock like one of those Russian wobbly dolls.'

'Don't be so dramatic,' Emily said with a raucous laugh. 'That's my province. Try to remember that Chad won't notice or care what you're wearing. To a love-blinded man you'll be gorgeous if you're dressed in a paper bag. If someone asks him about your dress afterwards all he'll be able to recall is that you wore something white with a veil.'

'We'll work something out I promise,' Louise assured her. It would be her biggest failure if Maggie didn't feel beautiful walking down the aisle next Saturday. 'I'm going to pour us both a stiff drink before I tell you everything I achieved this morning, with a lot of help from Chad's parents I must say.'

'I'll leave you to it.' Emily gave her sister a quick hug and hurried off.

'Gin? Vodka? Whisky?' Louise asked. 'Name your poison.'

'All of the above?' Maggie suggested with a wry smile

'I don't think that's a good idea. As little as you're eating these days it'll go straight to your head.'

'Sounds good to me.'

Louise laughed and fixed them both

a large gin and tonic. 'Right. Here's what we've done already.'

* * *

'Did you kidnap my brother and leave a male model behind?'

'Oh, for Christ's sake, it's only a haircut and a few new clothes,' Josh scoffed. 'I promised Mom I'd spruce up a bit before your big day.'

Chad laughed. 'I guess it's got nothing to do with a certain blonde Englishwoman whose name rhymes with please?'

'Don't talk crap.'

'It's all right.' He slapped Josh's shoulder. 'My mouth is sealed although anyone with eyes and half a brain can see it written in neon lights above the pair of you.'

'You're full of bull.'

'Nope, you are big brother.'

Josh settled on silence as his best offence.

'Hey, when I called from Cornwall to

61

talk about Maggie you mentioned a woman who broke your heart and promised to tell me about her.'

'Don't you forget *anything*?' Josh groused. 'Damn lawyers. You must have sponges for brains.'

'You weren't by any chance talking about Ellen Carter?'

Josh didn't answer.

'Our folks never said much in my hearing because little pitchers have big ears I guess but — '

'You were a monkey for listening at doors.'

Chad shrugged. 'Hey I might've only been eight but I wasn't dumb. I knew she was your girlfriend and then suddenly she wasn't and you scarpered. I'm still waiting. You gonna 'fess up?'

'You'll have a long wait.' Josh glanced at the clock on the wall. 'I've gotta go.'

'You got a hot date lined up?'

'Nope. I'm meeting Louise to talk about *your* wedding plans.' Chad had the decency to look ashamed and Josh quickly seized the advantage. 'If you're not careful your bachelor send-off will be a tea party complete with dainty sandwiches and those dumb one bite fancy cakes.'

'You're as doomed as I was when I met Maggie.' Chad grinned. 'Anyway no self-respecting tea room would let you over the threshold.' His gaze swept down over Josh. 'You know what they say about not making a silk purse out of a sow's ear.'

Too near the knuckle, bro.

'I'm only kiddin', you know that, right?'

'Sure.'

'I didn't — '

'Drop it,' Josh begged.

'I appreciate all you're doin' — '

'Forget it. Not a problem.' He didn't do well with gratitude. In the military no one expected praise for doing their duty and deep down that's what this was.

'I'm serious.' Chad's eyes narrowed. 'I asked a lot of you to come home for the whole week.'

Yeah, you damn well did. 'Just make sure you stick with Maggie so I never have to do this again.' His brother's stony expression told Josh his attempt at humour failed miserably. 'My turn to say I'm kidding.'

'Yeah, and mine to say 'sure' and not mean it,' Chad tossed back. 'Seriously I'm not interested in any sort of bachelor party. We both know I've made the most of being single and the novelty wore off years ago.'

'Have you boys seen your father?' Their mother bustled into the room. 'He promised he'd quit work early. All of your cousins are coming over tonight for a barbecue.' She stopped talking and stared at Josh. 'Oh, sweetheart, don't you look handsome? You'll be beating off all the single women at the wedding.'

Josh forced on a half-hearted smile. 'Yeah right, Mom. Sorry to split and run but I've got to track down Louise for a wedding plan summit.' He made a quick retreat from the room and guessed he'd be the topic of conversation as soon as he was out of earshot.

He discovered Louise on the screened porch and as soon as he opened the door a flush of pink heat tinted her creamy skin as her gaze swept over him.

'Don't you start,' he warned. 'I've had it up to here from Mom and Chad already. I got a haircut and bought a few new clothes. No big deal. End of story.'

Louise covered her mouth with her hand and mumbled.

'Yeah yeah very funny I'm sure.' Josh dropped down into the chair next to her. 'So, what've you done today?' He couldn't decipher her muttered reply but the sparkle in her eyes gave away how much she was enjoying this. 'Quit it, woman, and talk to me.'

'That's far more like the gruff soldier I know and . . . like.'

'Gotta live up to my reputation. I bumped into Emily earlier and you've done a bang up job there. She's well on track with the additional food.'

'Yes, she is now but things were a little dicey earlier,' Louise confessed. 'Maggie and Emily crossed swords and I managed to defuse the situation before we ended up with a repeat of the Cornish smashed wedding cake disaster.'

'Well done. I had a few awkward moments at Cheekwood when I went to check on the venue. Last night I had an off-the-wall idea and wanted to scope out the spaces we've booked for the ceremony and reception.' He caught her flash of panic. 'Don't fret there's no problem with either. The contract Chad and Maggie signed bans any other catering outside of the vendors on Cheekwood's approved list. That would stop us using Emily's food, but it's all sorted now. I worked my charms on Miss Kathy, the event coordinator who happens to be an old friend of my mom. Thank God they were at school together back in the day.'

'Well isn't it just wonderful that dear Miss Kathy was happy to break the rules for us?'

Louise's sarcastic response took him aback. 'Hey, I did exactly what you asked. What's the problem?'

7

If Louise explained how her ex-boss used his power and influence to take advantage of her would it change things with Josh in a good or bad way? She hadn't mentioned Craig Merton's name to anyone except Audrey in the last five years and even with her employer she'd edited the unpleasant truth. The last thing she wanted was Josh or anyone else seeing her as a victim.

'It pisses you off doesn't it? The whole name-dropping money thing.' Louise couldn't decide whether to laugh or cry at how close he was to the truth. 'I understand more than you realise. It's one reason I got on well in the military. When you're under fire no one gives a shit whether you're a millionaire or from the wrong side of the tracks. Bullets don't discriminate.'

She couldn't speak.

'I'm takin' a wild guess you've been messed around by someone rich and powerful?' Josh leaned over and picked up her hand. 'Me too.' He tightened his grasp. 'My father in case you hadn't guessed.'

The hitch in his voice brought tears to her eyes and Louise fought down the urge to pour out everything. Years of self-control kicked back in and she pulled her hand away. Louise wasn't stupid. Today's smart clothes and sharp haircut didn't change the essence of who Josh really was but they did crystallise her dangerous, unwelcome reaction to him.

'I'm sorry.' She hurried to apologise.

'What for?'

'Being so rude. You've done a great job and I'm sure Maggie and Chad will be thrilled.'

'There, it didn't kill you to thank me, did it?' Josh's eyes sparkled.

'Don't talk nonsense.'

He shifted his chair closer and Louise started to babble about the wedding dress issue and the cut-back in

Maggie's social engagements until she ran out of words.

'Well done.' A wry smile tugged at the corners of his mouth. '*I* don't mind giving praise where it's due.'

'I ought to go.' Louise ignored his pointed comment. 'Audrey may need help changing for dinner.'

'I'm not stopping you.'

Perhaps I want you to.

'If you haven't caught on already that's not how I do things. I don't play games.' The sad edge to his voice tore at Louise. 'I'd better go as well.' Josh rose from the chair and loomed over her. 'Apart from standing up with Chad at his wedding I'm *nobody's* best man — trust me.' His scathing words sliced right through her but she stayed silent as he left.

★ ★ ★

Josh took the stairs two at a time. For both their sakes he needed to get away from Louise and fast. He'd endured

70

enough himself to recognise pain in another person — the type buried so deep it could almost be forgotten until one small trigger blew it all apart. In his case it could be as simple as a Fourth of July firework exploding too close to him or hearing the heart-wrenching lyrics of a particular song. Josh ached to know her story but couldn't imagine sharing his own in return. Even in therapy he'd largely held back but he wasn't alone, in fact the opposite. In one particular session, out of ten veterans, only two of them spilled their guts completely. *Yeah, and they're the ones making a whole life now while the rest of us drag around our fears and regrets like a goddamn lead weight.*

In his bedroom he unbuttoned his shirt and yanked it off before kicking his shoes to the opposite side of the room and removing his new trousers. Josh tugged on his oldest pair of jeans and a ratty black T-shirt before shoving his feet into an old pair of leather sandals. Grabbing his car keys and wallet he cracked the door open a couple of inches and headed out.

Half way down the stairs two sharp knocks on the front door brought him to a halt. Josh glanced around and waited for Betty Lou or his mother to appear but they were nowhere in sight. Reluctantly he flung open the door and froze as the big blue eyes long etched into his memory latched onto him. Ellen Carter, the woman who'd broken his eighteen-year-old heart, stared back in shock.

'Wow, Josh, I didn't expect you to be here.'

'Why not?' He struggled to contrast this sophisticated, mature woman with the slip of a girl who'd worshipped him twenty plus years ago.

'Are you back for good or just for the wedding?'

He gave a slight shrug and didn't answer.

'I heard you moved out west with no intention of ever returning to Nashville.'

'You shouldn't listen to rumours.'

Ellen held out an elaborately wrapped box decorated with a flamboyant silver bow. 'My folks meant to bring this gift over for Maggie and Chad before they went off on a Caribbean cruise but didn't have time so I offered . . . I wouldn't have come — '

'You don't need to apologise Ellie, it's been half a lifetime.' She flinched at Josh's use of his old pet name for her. 'The past is the past. We've both moved on.' He'd spent over twenty years wondering what might have been and now felt only a disinterested curiosity about his old girlfriend. 'How's life been treating you?'

'Awesome. I married Will Harding.' She waved around a set of flashy diamond rings. 'He took over his father's business and now he's president and CEO of Harding's Heavenly Cookies. We've got two adorable sons, Will Junior and Robson.' She gave a patently fake laugh. 'In fact I'd better head home before they run rings around the poor babysitter.'

'Who was at the door?' His father emerged from his study. 'Ah, Ellen, good to see you. It's been a while. How're your mom and dad?'

'Cruising again.' Ellen laughed. 'They spend more time at sea these days than anywhere else.'

'I'll take that if you like.' Big J held out his hands for the box. 'I'm sure Chad and Maggie will appreciate the thought.' He angled Josh a sharp glance. 'You weren't going out?'

He ignored the question. No way was he getting in an argument with his father in front of Ellen.

'Maybe I'll see you around, Josh,' she ventured.

'Maybe.' He opened the door. 'Thanks for coming.'

'It was my pleasure.'

For a fleeting second they held each other's gazes before Josh broke eye contact first. 'Goodbye, Ellen.' The second he closed the door his father laid into him.

'You were goin' to sneak out, weren't

you? So much for all that bull about supporting your brother.'

'It's only dinner, not the damn wedding.'

'Yeah. A *family* dinner. Do you even understand what the word means?' His father persisted. 'Your mom keeps harping on to me about being *kind* to you. More *understanding*. I think it's about damn time you did something for us in return.'

Josh remembered the strategy from one of the army counsellors for coping with stressful situations and steadied himself with a couple of deep breaths. 'Whether you believe it or not I have been making an effort but I'm sorry if it's not enough. I'm going for a quick drive but I'll be back to join you for dessert. And don't worry I'll change clothes for Chad and Maggie's sake. And Mom's.' A flash of pain shadowed his father's deep set eyes.

'I did you and that girl a favour all those years ago.' Big J blustered. 'We both know if you married Ellen it wouldn't have lasted. You were kids. Somebody needed to give the two of you a reality check.'

The sharp observation stuck in Josh's throat.

'She'd been spoiled rotten by her folks growin' up and it suits her that Will Harding's rolling in money and likes flashing it around. That girl wouldn't have lasted five minutes as an army wife. No backbone.' He gave Josh a shrewd stare. 'Your mama reckons we clash because we're too much alike.'

'Alike? Us?'

'She's a smart cookie. You think I ride roughshod over her but that's crap. She and I both know who's in charge and it's sure as heck not me.' His father chuckled but Josh couldn't let down his guard enough to join in. 'By the way I got in touch with a guy I know at one of the local community colleges and I've lined up some help for Maggie.'

'In what way?'

'Don't be so goddamn suspicious.' Big J frowned. 'You're not the only one who wants this wedding to go off well.'

'Sorry.' The word stuck in Josh's throat. 'What have you got?' He listened in amazement as his father explained that he'd arranged for two of the top students in the culinary arts programme to work as Maggie's assistants for the next few days.

'Graduation was last week and summer classes don't start until the end of the month so we can make use of the college kitchens which are a heck of a lot larger than ours. It gives the students valuable experience and a pay cheque while taking some of the burden off Maggie.'

'That's . . . awesome.'

'You changin' your mind and stayin' for dinner?'

Josh couldn't refuse.

'Don't be late.'

Back upstairs he hesitated outside Louise's door as the idea of apologising flitted through his head and out again. Josh decided to stick to a cold shower instead.

8

'We aren't going down to dinner until you tell me what your young man said to upset you,' Audrey persisted. 'You flew up here so fast I thought the Hound of the Baskervilles was chasing you. Ever since you've stomped around the room and snapped at me every time I try to speak. If I wasn't such a compassionate employer I'd fire you.'

They both knew Audrey had no intention of getting rid of Louise. 'Josh Robertson is *not* my young man and never will be.' She ignored the mischievous sparkle in Audrey's pale blue eyes. 'We simply had a difference of opinion over the wedding plans.'

'Did he fail on the tasks you gave him? I'm surprised.'

Louise couldn't allow Audrey to think badly of Josh. After going over and over it in her head she'd come to the conclusion she'd overreacted. She calmly set the record straight and waited to be told off.

'Sometimes you are a very silly girl,' Audrey bemoaned. 'Joshua seems like an intelligent man. He asked for answers you wouldn't give him. Am I right?'

Louise nibbled at her lower lip.

'I can get it out of him you know. Oddly enough he and his brother both enjoy talking to me.' Audrey preened.

'I can't stop you asking him,' Louise conceded. 'I've got far bigger problems at the moment.'

'I know you successfully got rid of the dress Maggie hated but I take it you're still searching for a replacement? I can talk to my goddaughter if — '

'No.' Louise cut her off. 'I promised I wouldn't let you interfere.'

'In that case I'll keep my brilliant idea to myself. I won't mention the very interesting conversation I had yesterday with Mrs Robertson.'

She might as well get it over with or

her employer would toy with her for the rest of the day. 'I give in. Amaze me.'

'The Robertson family are all avid collectors whether it's antiques, china or guitars. You might be interested to know that Tricia Robertson's particular passion lies in vintage clothing.'

Louise clung onto her waning patience.

'She inherited trunks full of beautiful family clothing and showed me a particularly fine example belonging to her grandmother.'

'Very interesting.'

'What era particularly fascinates Chandler?' Audrey persisted.

'Art Deco. Early 1920s up to the beginning of the Second World War. The same as you.'

'Would you care to guess when Tricia's grandmother was married?'

'I'd hate to spoil your fun. Why don't *you* tell *me*?' Her arch reply made Audrey laugh.

'1925.'

'What a surprise. Don't tell me — let me guess — Mrs Robertson owns her grandmother's wedding dress.'

'Maybe you should ask her yourself? I wouldn't want to *interfere*.'

'You knew this was my worst problem didn't you?' Louise beamed and impulsively reached over to give Audrey a kiss. A tinge of colour highlighted Audrey's sunken cheeks and the tiniest of smiles curved her thin lips. 'I'll ask Tricia if I can take a look at it and cross my fingers the style will work on Maggie.'

'Of course the wedding dress is a relatively simple problem compared to Joshua,' Audrey observed. 'He needs a little working on but the right woman could tackle him and end up with a decent man.'

She didn't answer and the silence drew out between them until for once Louise won.

'Help me up.' Audrey held out her hand and eased off of the sofa. 'After dinner you can leave me to amuse the family while you sort things out with Joshua.' Her piercing gaze swept over

Louise. 'You should change before we go down. That grey dress does nothing for you.'

'That's unfortunate because it's what I'm wearing.' *I do have some pride.*

★ ★ ★

Josh snagged two beers and wended his way around a crowd of noisy children playing tag on the lawn. 'Hey, little brother, want one?' He held out a bottle to Chad.

'Thanks.' Chad popped the top and took a long drink before wiping his mouth. 'Dad says you had a visitor earlier.'

'Correction. You did. Ellen Carter, or Harding I guess she is now, brought over a wedding present for you and your lovely bride.'

'She is lovely, isn't she?' Chad gazed fondly over at Maggie, holding a sleeping Rose in her arms and rocking the baby with a dreamy look on her face.

'Yeah, she sure is. You struck gold there. You'll be a father yourself before you know where you are,' Josh teased.

'I sure hope so. How about you?'

'Me?' Josh choked on a mouthful of beer. 'Heck. Don't do that again unless you want to kill me off.'

'The idea of settling down used to freak me out too.' Chad grinned. 'You wanna talk about Ellen?'

'Nope.'

Chad scowled. 'You and Dad are so damn alike. Stubborn as mules the pair of you.'

That was the second time today he'd heard the same bizarre claim. 'You know Ellen and I were high school sweethearts and in our own dumb way we kind of got unofficially engaged until Dad stuck his oar in and broke us up. End of story.'

'And today?'

Josh frowned. 'I put it to rest. I'm relieved she came.'

'Now you're free to go after your heart.'

'Oh, for Christ's sake, Chad, stop talking like Oprah.' Josh shook his head in fake disgust.

'She keeps looking over this way.'

'Who does?'

Chad rolled his eyes. 'Your admirer. The one with the cut-glass accent and killer legs.'

'Killer legs? You're almost a married man, bro.'

'Hey, I'm engaged not dead. No harm in lookin'.' Chad chuckled. 'Anyway Maggie's are hotter. I homed in on them the first day although they were buried underneath her ugly green dress. Louise's dreary grey thing is a fashion statement in comparison.'

'What sort of look am I getting anyway? Poisonous or pissed off?' Josh quipped. 'We didn't part on good terms earlier.' Before he could think better of it he poured out the whole story and his brother listened quietly.

'You dick.'

'Cheers pal. Good to know I can always rely on you,' Josh retorted.

'You manoeuvred Louise into a corner. I thought you'd know better than that from your army days.'

Josh took another long draw of beer. 'So how would you've handled it, hot shot?'

'I'd have changed the subject then confessed a few of my own screw-ups.' Chad grinned. 'I'm sure you'd have plenty to choose from.'

A whole truckload but he didn't intend on going into any details. 'The timing is lousy.'

'Always is, bro. You think Maggie and I had it easy? Boy, I had to work hard for that woman. Literally. I spent most of our cousin's wedding reception helping her pass off a destroyed cake as something worth eating. Emily wasn't much help. She kept messing up her own life and Maggie's by behaving like a spoiled brat. I also had to convince Maggie that she was worth loving.' Chad shook his head. 'Then there's all the baggage I hauled around. I'd started to buy into my reputation as

Nashville's most eligible bachelor until Maggie pulled me down a peg or two. While you mull all that over, go get me another beer.' He winked. 'If you're smart you'll make your way to the kitchen via the shade garden instead of taking the direct route.'

Audrey, their mother and all the aunts were congregated on comfortable wicker chairs under the canopy of several large oak trees. They were surrounded by beds full of Tricia's prized shade-loving hosta plants in the semi-private garden. Louise was flitting around talking to everyone and helping to refill drinks from a table set up in one corner.

'Offer to help. Charm the older women.' Chad smiled. 'Audrey is the key. Get her on your side and you'll be in.'

In what? More trouble?

'One more piece of advice for what it's worth. Try smiling. Right now you've got your don't-mess-with-me face on like you're heading into combat.'

Josh nodded and forced on a smile. 'Force of habit.' When a person spent months on end with little respite from the stress of wondering if they'd see another sunrise it didn't come easy to shuck that off and be 'normal' again.

'I get it.' Chad hesitated. 'Tell me about it sometime over a few more beers? I'm not a kid any more.'

'Yeah, I know.'

'Good luck.' Chad gave him a shove. 'Don't forget my beer.'

His brother was about to marry an amazing woman. Josh was on his own. Maybe for once Chad knew something he didn't.

9

'Wow!' Trisha's older sister Sally exclaimed. 'Josh sure is looking good.'

'I can't take all the credit. Try asking someone standing not a million miles away from us.'

Louise's cheeks burned but she ignored the pointed remark. 'Mrs Robertson, I mean Tricia, could we have a wedding dress summit later? I purposely haven't mentioned our idea to Maggie because I'd love it to be a surprise.'

'Sure, hon.'

'Hi, ladies, how are y'all doin'?'

Josh's deep, delicious drawl insinuated itself into Louise's brain.

'Don't you ever stop working?'

'I'm not here on holiday.'

'Anything I can do to help?'

'You've done enough.' A rush of embarrassing heat flared up her neck and Louise felt all the women watching them. Josh's rich warm laughter trickled into her heart.

'How about you take a walk with me tonight and we'll talk.' A wicked smile tugged at the corners of his tempting mouth. 'Yeah, I know the words talk and me don't often go together but I'll give it a try.'

Louise wasn't sure exactly what he had in mind, or maybe she did and the idea scared her. 'I won't be free until quite late. After the barbecue is finished Maggie, Tricia, Emily and I are having a wedding dress session.' She glanced over her shoulder to make sure Maggie wasn't listening. 'Our bride-to-be still thinks she's wearing the meringue I told you about but we've got a surprise for her.'

'Don't tell me — it's an apple pie.' Josh leaned close and whispered in her ear. 'With smooth, silky vanilla ice cream melting all over the hot crust.'

'Behave,' she hissed.

'Joshua, stop flirting with my assistant and come over here,' Audrey ordered. 'I should like to try one of the hot dogs.'

'Okay but you'll have to hold it in your hands to eat. No knives and forks allowed even for Brits.'

Louise suppressed a giggle as the old woman fixed Josh with her sternest glare. 'In case you're not aware an Englishman, the Earl of Sandwich, invented the original hand-held food. I believe I can manage perfectly well. I'm not the ancient relic you seem to believe I am.'

'I'll go fetch you one.' He caught Louise's eye and gave her a long, slow wink before strolling away with a distinct swagger.

Oh boy was she ever in trouble.

★ ★ ★

'You gave my wedding dress away?' Maggie shrieked. 'Are you mad? I'll be walking down the aisle naked. Wonderful.'

'Calm down.' Emily pushed her sister down on the sofa. 'Of course we all

90

know one man who'd be ecstatic if that occurred but he's going to be out of luck. You asked Louise to change the dress you hated and she's succeeded.'

'But I didn't ask her to — '

'Be quiet and listen to what she's trying to tell you.'

Louise crossed her fingers behind her back before opening her mouth to speak. If Maggie didn't love their idea she'd be sunk. 'I've got to give all the credit to Audrey. She put together a conversation she had with Trisha and your wedding dress problem. I'm sure you'll love the solution and Chad will be over the moon.' *Always sound confident even when you aren't.* She'd used the same method in many different situations including the day she'd turned the tables on a man who considered himself invincible where women were concerned. 'Tricia, why don't you explain?'

Maggie's sceptical expression altered as she listened to her future mother-in-law's mesmerising story about her grandmother, coincidentally another Margaret, and her wedding dress.

'Originally it was ivory but with age it's turned a far deeper shade almost verging on blush. The dress is made of silk chiffon and satin. There's a gorgeous satin belt and the most exquisite beading.'

'It sounds absolutely beautiful but be realistic, Tricia.' Maggie sighed. 'I don't have the straight up and down figure for the 1920's styles.'

'The first Margaret didn't either so it was specially designed to suit her by giving a hint of curves in the shape while retaining the fashion of the day. I had it professionally restored about five years ago in the hope someone would wear it again one day.' Tricia patted Maggie's hand. 'It never occurred to me to offer it to you before because I took it for granted you'd want something new and showy. That was really dumb on my part because you're not that way.' She gave a wry smile. 'I guess I kind of projected onto you what I wished *my* daddy could afford when *I got* married. We didn't have a lot of money and he was too proud to accept any help from Joshua's family. Will you at least let us show you Margaret's dress?'

Louise seized on the bride's temporary silence and hurried into the other room to unhitch the dress from the front of the wardrobe. She gave the fragile material a wistful glance before carrying the dress back into the other room with a bright smile.

'Oh, Louise.' Maggie's deep blue eyes shone with happy tears.

Bingo.

★ ★ ★

'I wish you could've seen her face.' Louise sighed.

It couldn't be any lovelier than yours. Josh was sure Louise would call him too smooth for his own good if he dared to say such a thing out loud.

'We've got a seamstress coming in the morning to make a few alterations but it's already close to perfect on Maggie.'

'Chad will bawl like a baby when he sees her.' Josh laughed. 'He's into showing his emotions in his old age.'

'Considering you're even more ancient shouldn't you be crying non-stop?'

'Yeah, well, some of us have more self-control.'

'And is that working out well?'

'About as well as it is for you.' Josh regretted his rudeness as every drop of colour drained from Louise's face. 'Sorry. I didn't bring you out here to insult you.'

They'd slipped away when everything quietened down and walked through the park for a while, making the most of the pale moonlight along the paved trail. Josh found himself talking about the history of the Robertson land and for once didn't try to cover up his pride in the family.

'Really? What you did bring me out here for?' Louise's voice trembled.

'All I wanted was to talk. We never get a minute alone.' Josh stroked her hair, let free tonight from its usual tight knot and hanging loose around her shoulders. 'I want — '

'What do you want?' Louise whispered.

'I lead a solitary life these days and most of the time it works.' Josh struggled on. 'But you make me want more.'

'You do the same for me but trust me I'm not looking for that either.'

Louise dropped her head to rest against his chest and he automatically wrapped his arms around her, acutely aware of her tempting scent and the way she fitted into every curve of his body. 'We've only got five days. After the wedding you'll head back to Colorado and I'll fly back to England.'

'You think we'll be able to simply shake hands and say goodbye?' Josh scoffed. 'We both keep a protective layer of caution wrapped around us and it takes a lot to crack through.' His observation brought back her smile. 'My excuse is the twenty years I spent in the army when I planned ahead, carefully thought things through, reacted swiftly when necessary but always kept certain unbreakable rules in the forefront of my mind. What made *you* the way you are?'

'I can't talk about it.'

'Can't or won't?' he persisted.

'Does it matter?'

Josh cupped her face with his hands and shoved his fingers up through her silky hair. 'Everything about you matters to me.'

'Would 'can't at the moment but willing to try later' satisfy you?' Her luminous dark eyes smouldered.

'Yeah, if I can say the same right back at you? I get this isn't a one-way street.'

'We're making progress.' Her light tone didn't fool him. 'Perhaps we ought to go back to the house.'

'Not yet.'

'Why not?'

'Because if we hurry we'll miss this.' Josh drew her closer and lowered his mouth to hers. He swept his tongue across her soft lips and a tiny moan escaped the back of her throat before he pulled away. 'I'd better get you home. We'll work things out.'

'Do you really think so?'

'Of course. Trust me.'

Louise's smoky gaze lingered. 'I really want to.'

He didn't push her. *Can't at the moment but willing to try later.* That would do for tonight.

10

'By the way what are *you* wearing?' Maggie twirled and admired herself in the mirror. The vintage dress gleamed and shimmered under the lights, gently skimming Maggie's curves in such a perfect way it could've been designed for her.

'Wearing?' Louise frowned. 'When?'

'To my wedding, silly.'

'I've got a simple navy dress that — '

'Stop right there.' Maggie held up her hand. 'Don't tell me. It's obviously the equivalent of my infamous green dress.'

'What on earth are you talking about?' She'd heard about the notorious dress but couldn't see its connection to her.

'I wore the same ugly green dress to every wedding I worked or went to as a guest for years.' Maggie's cheeks flamed. 'Chad worked out I used it as a sort of hair shirt because I didn't think I was pretty enough to deserve better. I'd been carrying around a lot of guilt because Emily always blamed me for our mother's death and we needed to get past that before I could truly be myself.'

Louise didn't intend to dump her own problems on Maggie. 'You're reading far too much into this,' she insisted. 'Let's be honest. You really only invited me because Audrey brought me along to help her out. My dress is perfectly smart enough and I won't let you down in front of the Robertsons' wealthy friends.'

'That wasn't what I meant and you know it,' Maggie protested and an enigmatic smile pulled at the corners of her mouth. 'Oh, you're clever. You think by implying I've turned into a fashion snob you can weasel out of giving me an honest answer.' She spread her hands over her generous hips and tossed her mass of unruly brown hair. 'Do you honestly think Chad's marrying me for my dress sense?'

Louise gave a slight shrug. She'd almost told Josh the truth last night but in the end something held her back. *Trust.* She wasn't certain she could trust him and for that same reason she'd never had any close female friends. When people shared their feelings and secrets they usually expected the same in return.

For a minute Maggie didn't speak. She took off the wedding dress and carefully hung it back up. 'It's time for Cinderella to go back into the kitchen. Chad's father has been wonderful and he's lined up a couple of incredible local culinary students to help me. We finished one of the cakes yesterday and if I get the second one baked this morning before the bridal luncheon I should be on track. Nick and Suzy will help me decorate them early tomorrow morning. Luckily there's plenty of space to store everything there at the college when we're done which makes it so much easier.' She pulled on a pair of stretchy black leggings and a loose pink tunic before scraping her hair back and securing it with an elastic band. 'Join me.'

'But I'm not a cook and I've . . . got things to do. Audrey — '

'Can wait an hour.' Maggie's decisive manner startled Louise. 'My sister's busy with Jonathan and the baby. We can pour our hearts out to each other and no one need ever know.' Louise's horror must have shown because Maggie burst into peals of laughter. 'Don't fret. I'm joking. I won't forget we're both well brought up English girls who aren't used to spilling their guts — that's such a nasty expression, don't you think?'

'I suppose so,' she muttered.

Maggie grabbed her arm. 'Come on. You can grease and line the cake tins under supervision while I mix the batter. That way we don't have to look at each other while we chat.'

Louise hid her inner grimace with a half-hearted smile. 'Lead the way.'

'You're not Marie Antoinette setting off to her execution.'

At least the French queen knew it'd be over with quickly.

'I'm serious, Josh, I don't want one.'

Josh stared at his brother. 'You're only sayin' that because you know I'm useless at all this social crap. I made you a promise and I'll keep it if it kills me.'

'Open your damn ears for once. I don't want a bachelor party.'

'Why not?' he persisted. If Josh didn't know better he'd swear Chad was blushing.

'Bachelor parties imply the groom is reluctant to abandon his single life and I'm not.'

'You're readin' too much into it.'

'Maybe.' Chad gave him a long, hard stare. 'We both grew up extremely privileged. You escaped it your way but I revelled in the whole shebang for too long. Work ground me down and I wasted the evenings at a bunch of social events with people I mostly didn't give a damn about. At the end of a long day there wasn't anybody to talk with and look out for. Surely you get it?'

The tears pressing at the back of his eyes prevented Josh answering.

'I can't wait to be Maggie's husband and I'm not gonna pretend otherwise.' Chad shrugged. 'Anyway, she doesn't have enough girlfriends in Nashville for a party of her own so this evens things up.'

'You swear you're not doing this for my sake?'

'Get your head out of your butt. I'm not that nice, bro.'

'True.'

'Are you making any progress with the lovely Louise?'

Josh didn't appreciate the implication behind Chad's question.

'Don't bite my head off. Anyone can see the sparks between the two of you. Audrey warned me off toying with Maggie the day we met and I told her I admired Maggie very much and 'messing around' wasn't on my agenda.'

'Yeah, well, I'll take a leaf out of your book and say the same.'

Chad's face creased into a devilish smile. 'Here's a bit of advice you can either take or tell me to shove where the sun don't shine — don't drag your heels too long. Women only find the stoic, macho, real-men-don't-cry persona attractive in small doses.'

'But?'

'She'll want more.'

'What if *I* want more and I'm not getting it,' Josh retorted. 'And before you turn all smart-ass on me I'm not talkin' about sex.'

'Whoa. Why don't you tell me what we *are* talking about here?' Chad frowned.

'I'm not sure because Louise is as closed up as I am.'

'Wonderful. Brick wall meets brick wall. This is gonna work out great.'

Josh had come to the same conclusion the night before when he couldn't sleep.

'Rushing Louise won't do any good.'

'Aren't you the smart one?' Josh jibed. 'It's a damn good thing our folks spent a fortune on your fancy Vanderbilt law school education.'

'At least I'm not burying myself in some godforsaken part of the country because I don't have the guts to face up to real life.' Chad blanched. 'Hey, I'm sorry,' he apologised, 'I should never have said that.'

'Why not? You obviously thought it. You haven't got a goddamn clue.'

'Yeah. So tell me.' Chad challenged. 'Oh, no, I forgot. You prefer the whole martyr thing.'

'Keep the noise down, boys.' Big J strode into the room, glaring at them both. 'Your mother's got enough on her plate without hearing you two arguing like little kids. Jack it in right now. We've got an agreement, remember?' He rested a hand on Chad's shoulder. 'I'm heading into work. You coming?'

'I guess but we've got to pick up our tuxedos this afternoon so I'll be quitting early.'

'Do you want me to meet you at the store?' Josh offered.

'Sure. Three o'clock and don't be late.'

He managed a tight smile. 'I don't do late. I'm sorry about . . . you know. We okay?'

'Of course we are, you moron.'

They left him alone and Josh decided to track Louise down and offer his help. It didn't matter what outlandish thing she asked him to do if he could simply spend time with her.

'Ah, there you are.' Louise popped her head around the door and Josh considered looking around for the genie he must've let out of the bottle. Conjuring her out of his imagination was pretty amazing even for him. 'You're coming shopping with me.'

'Um, sure, what are we after? English stuff for the reception?' She'd mentioned the possibility of adding a few things to the wedding decor and they'd tossed some ideas around. 'Betty Lou told me about a place out on West End that does — '

'Maybe later,' she interrupted. 'First we're going dress shopping.'

'I don't have the legs for it.' Josh grinned. 'They're too hairy. Chad's getting us tuxedos. Much safer.' She stared as if he'd grown a third head.

'A dress for me, you idiot. I'll prove Maggie wrong if it's the last thing I do.'

He usually considered himself quick to catch on but her bizarre statement made absolutely no sense.

'It's a long story.' Louise sighed.

'I've got all the time in the world.' He refused to make do with another half-truth even if it was in reference to a dress.

'Fine. If you insist.' In a cool, dispassionate tone she told him a convoluted story involving Maggie's family and the infamous green dress. 'She's comparing that to the navy one I'd planned to wear to the wedding although I don't have a clue why.'

'Is it prettier than the grey one?'

Louise rolled her eyes. 'What is it with everyone and my grey dress?'

'It makes you fade into the background and you're far too beautiful for that.' As the words tumbled out even the tips of his ears burned. 'Are you ready to go shopping?'

'How can you say something so . . . lovely and sweet and then switch back to mundane without catching your breath?'

'Can I get away with saying it's a guy thing?' Josh asked.

'Only because I want your help.'

'But why ask *me*? Me and fashion aren't on first name terms.'

'You won't be judgmental. You'll be honest but won't make snide remarks about the cut of a particular dress not working because my thighs are too muscular.'

The image she inadvertently placed in his head did nothing for Josh's libido.

'Stop it,' she whispered. 'Let's go.'

'Let's look on this as a way to get to know each other better.' Josh reached for her hand.

'And that's a good thing?'

'Yeah, at least I think so. Let's find out.'

Louise's tentative smile gave him hope that maybe for once he'd said the right thing.

11

'Sorry the transport's not fancy.' Josh opened the truck door. 'I didn't expect to be ferrying any ladies around on this trip.'

'You mean you've managed to entice other women into your luxurious vehicle?' Louise joked in an effort to allay her nervousness. Lingering memories of last night's rendezvous in the park made her body hum. 'It suits you.'

'Battered around the edges, in need of a paint job and a little rusty around the undercarriage?'

'You said it, not me. My thoughts ran more on the lines of unpretentious and hard-working.'

A wide grin creased his face. 'Hop in and we'll see if she'll start.'

'I hope we're still talking about the truck?'

'*You* are trouble.'

'Have you only now worked that one out, Mr Robertson?'

'Sweetheart, I knew you were a threat to my sanity the day I set eyes on you.' His delicious, low drawl made her skin suddenly too tight for her body.

'Shopping.' Louise's voice wobbled. 'Maggie said to try the Opry Mills mall first and only resort to the more expensive Green Hills one if I get desperate. Do you know where they both are?'

'Sure do, not that I've ever darkened the doors of either. When I was a kid the Opry Mills mall area was a cool theme park called Opryland and I used to beg my folks to take me there every weekend. I'm guessing it went out of business back in the late nineties.' Josh closed her door and ran around to settle himself in the driver's seat. 'It'll take us about thirty minutes to get there.'

'Perfect.' A lone butterfly wriggled around her stomach. 'Is it 'try later' confession time?'

'You go first. I'm driving.'

Louise pondered where to start while he got them headed towards Opry Mills. 'When I got the job with Audrey five years ago it saved me making an even bigger fool of myself.'

'Is that your opinion or everyone else's?'

'A bit of both.' She was already starting to regret her offer to be honest with Josh. 'My upbringing was very unstable to say the least. My mother had her first baby, my half-sister Jules, when she was a teenager and my grandmother raised her. My father abandoned my mother when she got pregnant with me and I've no idea if he's alive or dead. Mum struggled to keep things together when she had me but when I was fourteen she couldn't cope any longer and sent me to live with Jules. We'd hardly ever seen each other before that and poor Jules was married with a couple of young children of her own by that point. Having me dumped on her couldn't have been easy but she never complained.' Louise shook her head. 'I should've appreciated her more but I resented being there and kept running away. After I turned sixteen she stopped asking the police to fetch me back.'

'What happened to your mother?'

'I don't have a clue.' Louise admitted. 'Jules might know.'

'That's tough but you've obviously turned things around so you must've done somethin' right.'

Compliments made her uneasy and Louise shrugged it off. 'I went back to school and earned a few qualifications but couldn't afford to go on to university. I worked hard and didn't really have a personal life. I rarely let myself be distracted by any man.'

'I'd like to bet more than a few were distracted by you.' His wry words lightened the mood and she couldn't help smiling.

'You're a surprisingly good listener,' Louise observed.

'Better than I am at talkin'.'

'Maybe. We'll find out later,' she pressed on, anxious to get the worst part over with. 'I expect your father and

113

Chad know Craig Merton because he's an English ceramics expert.' Her heart thumped. 'I met Merton through my job at an art auctioneers and I couldn't believe my luck when he wanted me as his researcher and administrative assistant. He doubled my pay which meant I could afford my own flat in London and I had the opportunity to travel all over Europe with him for the three years we worked together. My life was amazing.'

'Until it wasn't?'

She blinked back tears. 'For a woman in her late twenties I was incredibly naive where men were concerned. I had never met any man like Craig before. He was handsome, urbane, well-educated and had beautiful manners. He led me to believe we had something special between us far beyond work. He said he loved me, said we had a future together. But it all crumbled.' Louise struggled to keep breathing. 'When I caught on to what he was really like underneath the smooth veneer he . . . turned on me. I discovered later he'd played the same game with at least two of his previous assistants but none dared to speak up.'

'I'm guessing you did.'

'Yes. For all the good it did.'

'I'm guessin' he had money, influence and came from a good family. People believed his story over yours.'

'Oh yes, the Mertons are an old Norfolk family. Craig always boasted he could trace his ancestors back to the Norman Conquest. No one considered him capable of the things I accused him of. People knew we'd been close and assumed I was nothing more than a spurned woman getting revenge on a decent man. They couldn't accept that Craig coerced several women who worked for him to keep quiet about his unethical business methods by whatever means he considered 'necessary'.' Louise brushed helplessly at the tears trickling down her face. 'The implication was that I must be at least partly to blame and maybe they're right.' Josh pulled the truck off on the side of the road and stopped before gently undoing her seat belt and pulling her into his arms. Louise wept out her frustration until her anger ebbed away.

'Look at me.' He tilted her chin to meet his angry gaze. 'They're not right. After you broke off your personal relationship he should've backed off. Audrey knows all this?'

'Not the details but she knows enough.' She nodded. 'Several years ago she quietly stopped doing business with Craig because she had her doubts about his ethics and integrity.'

'I knew I liked the old lady for a good reason,' Josh said, with a small smile.

'There's very little gossip in the Art Deco collector's world that escapes her. When she heard rumours about my troubles with Craig Audrey approached me and offered me a job. She'd been searching for someone to help her with her art collection but hadn't found the right person. Audrey's a proud woman but her arthritis is extremely painful and a lot of everyday tasks are hard for her. For whatever reason we instantly felt at ease with each other.'

'Did Merton . . . ever force himself on you?'

'He tried on the day I left, but he didn't succeed.' Louise eked out a faint smile. 'I kicked him where it hurts a man most.'

'Good.' His expression darkened. 'I'd do a heck of a lot worse if I got my hands on him.'

'I know, but he's not worth it.'

His clear, hazel eyes gleamed. 'If you change your mind just say.'

'I will. That's enough for now. There are dresses waiting for me.' Her feeble attempt to bring things back to normal faltered on a sob.

'There certainly are.' Josh touched her cheek. 'Pretty ones worthy of a beautiful woman who's done with hiding herself away.' He brushed the whisper of a kiss over her mouth. 'Right?'

'Right.' She repeated hesitantly. 'Right.' Louise's voice strengthened. 'Drive on.'

★ ★ ★

Josh struggled to forget the story she'd told him but it wasn't easy. 'Okay, I'm ready.' He parked outside the mall. 'Let's do this.'

'We're going shopping not going into battle,' she joked. 'Oh, I'm sorry, that wasn't tactful. I shouldn't compare anything to — '

'Don't apologise. I'm not an unexploded bomb to be tiptoed around.' Josh grinned. 'See, I can make jokes as well as take them.'

Two hours later he was ready to wave the white flag of surrender.

'There's only one more shop Maggie recommended that we've not been in yet.' Defeat threaded through her voice and he made the instant decision to step in.

'Not a problem but we'll tackle this one differently.'

'In what way?'

'I'm gonna choose the dresses and you'll try them on without arguing.'

118

'You?' A cursory sweep down over his crumpled chinos and plain blue shirt conveyed her lack of faith. 'Oh, what does it matter? No one's going to look at me on Saturday anyway. They'll all be watching Maggie which is exactly the way it should be.'

'I won't,' Josh declared. 'Don't I matter?'

Louise flushed. 'Of course.'

Before she could change her mind he seized her hand and steered her into the shop. Josh approached the first sales assistant he saw and explained what they were looking for.

'Sit down for a few minutes while I see what's on offer.' Josh pointed towards a chair.

'Minutes? It's not going to take you very long.'

'Nope. I know your figure and I know what I like. Should be straightforward.' Josh caught the assistant's amused smile as Louise turned beet-red.

'Fine.'

'Right, sir, come this way.'

Josh wondered what the hell he'd let himself in for. *You can do this. Focus on the mission.* He started on the first rail and thrust an occasional dress at the woman trailing along behind him. *Oh, yeah, this is it.* He fingered the rich dark red lace and smiled.

'An excellent choice.' The assistant nodded. 'You know the lady well.'

Not as well as I'd like to.

'Ma'am, if you'd like to come this way please.' The woman smiled at Josh. 'You can wait here and we'll come back out to get your opinion when she's ready.'

Louise's eyes widened at the sight of the armful of clothes. 'Are you sure you picked out enough?'

'Most are fillers. The lady knows the one.'

'The one?'

'Yeah.' He chuckled. 'Trust me, it'll be obvious.' Josh joined an older man waiting on his wife and noticed the veteran's designation on his baseball cap. 'Vietnam, sir?' Soon they were engrossed in swapping war stories and he was almost sorry when the man's wife came to drag him away.

'Sorry I took so long. I hope Harry hasn't bored you to death.' She gave a rueful smile. 'He forgets everyone doesn't want to hear about his exploits nearly fifty years ago.'

'No apology needed, ma'am.' Josh rushed to reassure her. He wasn't lying when he swore he'd enjoyed every minute.

The woman helped her husband to stand up, making sure he was steady on his feet before she let go of his arm and her loving gesture tugged at Josh's heart.

'Thank you for your service, sir.'

'You too.' Harry's comment made his wife look at him but she didn't say a word. 'We'd better be off. Come on, Paula.'

As they walked away hand in hand Josh settled back to wait.

'What do you think, sir?'

He glanced up and swore under his breath.

'Do you like it? I'm not sure it's me.' Louise ventured.

Oh, it's you all right. One hundred percent you. 'It's perfect,' he rasped. *You're perfect.*

She tentatively smoothed her hands down over the sheer lace-over-silk sheath and Josh itched to do the same. 'You don't think it's a bit . . . much?'

Somehow he managed to shake his head. If she didn't buy this dress he'd know for sure there wasn't a God. The rich colour reminded him of a fine merlot and enhanced the smokiness of her eyes, making a perfect foil for her ash-blonde hair. 'Trust me.' Something passed between them and he sensed they'd reached a crossroads.

'It will need new shoes, a bag and jewellery,' she warned.

'Not a problem but we'll get us some lunch first before I fall apart.'

'That doesn't appear very likely.' Louise's wry assessment made him smile again, something she achieved with increasing frequency. 'If I show the dress to Maggie and she doesn't think it's suitable I'll be bringing it back.'

Over my dead body. If necessary he'd bribe Maggie to get her on his side. 'Fair enough.' He must not have hidden his true feelings because she tossed him a mock glare. 'I suppose you'd better take it off . . . for now.'

With a brilliant smile Louise turned away and walked back towards the changing room with a new sensuous swing to her hips. Josh wasn't stupid enough to believe that Merton's lingering effect on Louise's self-confidence was gone for good but hopefully they'd made a start.

He couldn't wait until Saturday when he'd see her in the dress again and maybe out of it if he was very lucky. His grandmother's voice filled his head, instantly admonishing him. *For heaven's sake behave like a gentleman, Joshua.* Rose Ann Robertson would return from Florida tomorrow and no one saw through him like his needle-sharp grandmother. He'd better make the most of today.

12

The depth of longing in Josh's eyes shook her. When they'd eaten lunch and done the rest of her shopping he drove them back to the house and dashed off to meet Chad. Louise couldn't decide if she was sorry or relieved.

Needing company she wandered into the kitchen and Maggie glanced up from pouring batter into an oversized cake tin.

'Before you offer I don't want any help with this one. It's ours.' She blushed. 'You'll be pleased to hear I survived lunch today. Actually I enjoyed it.' Maggie gave a rueful smile. 'Sometimes you have to simply go with the flow.'

'You're right. Not always easy though, is it?'

'No.' She licked the spoon. 'How did your shopping expedition go?'

'I bought a dress but I'm having

second thoughts about it now.'

'Did Josh approve of it?' When Louise didn't reply she burst into giggles. 'Oh, my, you're in trouble.' Maggie's cornflower-blue eyes sparkled.

'What do you mean?'

'I remember buying a sexy new dress when we went to Holland House for our — '

'Dirty weekend?' Louise teased. A few weeks after Fiona and Peter's wedding she'd taken Audrey to visit an old cousin and her employer surprised everyone by inviting Chad and Maggie to stay at her house while she was away.

'Let's just say that we never got around to eating dinner that evening.'

Every inch of Louise's body heated. By the unguarded expression on Josh's face earlier his thoughts ran along the same lines.

'You can't live your life being scared.' Maggie sighed. 'I almost messed up my wedding by forgetting what's important and what really doesn't matter.' She rested her hand on Louise's arm. 'You hinted yesterday that you've been hurt by a man but he's only one man. They're not all the same.'

Louise's head understood that Maggie was right but her cautious heart still wavered.

'Go upstairs and put the dress on while I stick this in the oven and wash my hands. That's an order and you have to keep the bride-to-be happy.' A cheeky smile crept over her face. 'This is the part I absolutely love. Until Saturday everyone is treating me like a queen and I'm not sure I'll like returning to reality afterwards.' She playfully smacked her head. 'Oops, yes I am, because I'll be Chad's wife which will be infinitely better.'

Louise absentmindedly selected a raspberry from the glass bowl and popped it into her mouth. 'There's so much I don't know about Josh. How can I even think of — '

'There's no harm in thinking.' Maggie stopped her musing. 'He's a good man.' She glanced over her shoulder to make sure they weren't being overheard. 'He's pretty hot too. Kind of an older, more rugged version of my own dreamboat.'

'He is, isn't he?'

'Hurry up and put on that dress before I die of curiosity.' Maggie shooed her away.

Upstairs Louise studied herself in the mirror and tried to be objective. She still couldn't understand what put the fire in Josh's eyes. She walked carefully down the stairs in the sky-high black stilettos Josh had chosen to go with the dress.

'Wow!' Maggie beamed. 'No wonder you brought Josh to his knees.'

'You don't think it's too tight?' Louise tugged at the waist.

'Not at all. If I tried to wear it I'd resemble a sausage stuffed into a size-too-small casing but you've got the figure for it. It's feminine but sexy and those shoes make your legs look a mile long.'

'You don't want me to take it back?'

'Don't you dare. For a start Josh would never speak to me again.' Maggie's wry laugh filled the room.

On Saturday she'd need a stiff drink before the wedding. Louise didn't dare to think about what might happen after.

★　★　★

'You clean up pretty well.' Chad checked out Josh's tuxedo. 'Louise will turn weak at the knees.'

'Wait until you see her dress.'

'Hot?'

'Scalding.'

'I'll be too busy gazing at my bride.'

'Quite right too.' Josh's voice trailed away. 'I'm not sure I can do this.'

'What? Be my best man? Romance Louise? Consider moving back to Nashville?'

'How the hell — '

'I know you, bro.' Chad shrugged. 'Just because we've spent a lot of time apart we're still brothers and I understand you.'

'You got any advice?' For a few seconds there was an uneasy silence. 'Forget it.'

'It's not that but I don't want to say the wrong thing again.' He glanced around. 'Why don't we get rid of these penguin suits? Let's find a dark bar somewhere and sink a couple of cold ones?'

Josh grinned. 'Works for me.'

They soon tracked down the perfect place, a dive bar well off the tourist track that Josh remembered from his teenage days. Years ago it hadn't been fussy about asking for IDs from obviously underage drinkers.

'What've you told Louise about your past?' Chad asked.

'Not much. She doesn't know about Ellen.'

'What about Afghanistan? Iraq? Any of the other war zones you went to?'

Josh shook his head and grabbed a handful of peanuts from a bowl on top of the bar. He shoved them into his mouth while he bided his time.

'I'm guessin' you didn't mention the Distinguished Service Cross you were awarded either?'

'Nope. Saving one man isn't a big deal when six others didn't make it.'

Chad scoffed. 'I'm pretty sure it was a damn big deal to Paul Winters. Wasn't he a family man?'

'Yeah.' Josh hated being forced to remember what he saw as the biggest failure of his military career. The irony of getting a medal for it didn't escape him. 'Married with a couple of little ones. But the others who died were all fine men and I let them down.'

'Hey, you saved two kids from growing up without a father and a wife from becoming a widow. Give yourself some credit.'

Josh held his tongue. There wasn't any point in arguing.

'So what's Louise's bugbear with men? You keep dropping hints. I can keep my mouth shut if need be.'

'Fine.' He gave in and told Chad about her trouble with Craig Merton, skipping over the details.

'That sucks.'

'Sure does.'

'Do you think the family trust fund would freak her out?' Chad mused.

'Probably but there's a lot about me could do that to her.'

'You won't know until you try.'

Josh wished his brother wasn't so damn sharp. 'Couldn't you have stayed young and annoying?'

'You mean I'm not?'

'Get the drinks in.'

'Yes, sir.' Chad ducked to avoid Josh's half-hearted swipe. 'This is a first you know.'

'What is?'

'Us drinking together.' He fixed Josh with the same bright hazel eyes he saw reflected back at him from the mirror every morning. 'First off I was too young and then you weren't around.'

Josh pointed over his head. 'Do you see the lousy brother sign flashing in neon lights?'

'Hey, you're here now.'

A rush of unexpected emotion swamped him.

'Maggie and I only got serious when

we were honest with each other. You can't avoid it, bro, not if you want to make things work with Louise.'

'Yeah, I know.' Josh sighed. 'It's just goddamn hard.'

'You spent twenty years doing 'hard'.'

'In other words don't be a moron?'

Chad's expression softened. 'I never said it'd be easy. Maggie about ripped me to pieces.'

'But it was worth it in the end?' Josh needed reassurance. 'Your lady sure is a gem.'

'So is Louise.'

He couldn't help smiling. 'Yeah, she is. I've no clue why she's interested in me.'

'I've never worked out why Maggie loves me either but I'll happily take what I can get.'

'Not a bad plan.' Josh wasn't sure whether to stir up what got them to the point of thumping each other earlier. 'All that stuff you spouted this morning about burying myself away because I don't have the guts to live life — I don't get it. Last year when mom and dad urged me to stay in Nashville and work in the business you didn't exactly back them up. You didn't speak out against me either when I came up with the plan to go to Colorado.'

'Yeah, I know. You'd obviously gone through hell and needed peace and quiet. I'm just not convinced it's doing you any good now. Do you?'

Josh didn't know how to respond.

'You're fitting in fine this week and getting on with people.' He held up a hand to stop Josh from interrupting. 'I'm not claiming it's easy but you've never taken the easy way out before.'

'What about when I left at eighteen and didn't look back?'

'I'm pretty damn sure nothing about that was easy. Nobody told me anything at the time because I was too young but I heard you and Dad argue all the time and Mom crying.'

'God, I was a shit.' Josh sighed.

'No, a stubborn teenage boy who thought he knew everything.' Chad grinned.

'It's pretty much accepted that's par for the course and now I'm an old man of thirty I agree. Ever since Dad took me to the factory when I was five and let me help design my first guitar I loved everything about the business and couldn't wait to get old enough to work there. But I got pissed at you for clearing off and blamed Dad. I insisted on going to law school to show Dad he couldn't push me around either.'

'Are you glad you've made the change back now?'

'I sure am. Every day I love going to work. Seeing the craftsmanship involved in every instrument we make and being a part of continuing the Robertson guitar legacy is incredible. Doesn't get much better than that in my book.' Chad mused and shook his head. 'Enough about me. Are you seriously thinking of moving back?'

'It's occurred to me but . . . I can't join the business. Not because of you or Dad,' he added. 'It's simply not my thing.'

'I get that.'

'Money isn't the main issue. I've got a fair amount of savings but I need to do something meaningful. Otherwise . . . it's all been for nothing.'

Chad drained his beer. 'I've heard you playin' out on the porch a few times. I'm guessing you still do some song writing?'

'Yeah. So what?'

'There's been a lot in the news here recently about music therapy for veterans. They've got a programme at one of the local Veterans' Administration hospitals and I know the guy who runs it. I sat in on a session last month and it's cool. Professional musicians help troubled veterans to write songs that explore what's on their minds.' Chad fiddled with a beer mat. 'The Robertson land out in Leiper's Fork isn't doing a whole lot and it's peaceful and quiet.'

Josh listened closely, trying to be realistic but unable to help being drawn in to his brother's vision.

135

'You could pull down the old cabin and get planning permission to build a therapy centre. We know enough folks it wouldn't be a huge challenge to network among the music community and get them involved.'

'We could do a mixture of residential and day courses,' Josh suggested, thinking out loud.

'You don't think the idea's completely off the wall?'

'Maybe, but one reason the family business has stood the test of time is our ability to think outside the box. When all this wedding hoopla is over next week I'll check the idea out some more.'

'The folks will be pleased to hear you're not rushing off as soon as the confetti settles.' Chad gave Josh a sly nudge. 'How long is the lovely Louise staying?'

'I haven't asked,' he muttered.

'If you put a bug in mom's ear I'm pretty sure she could be persuaded to invite the Dragon Lady to stay on a tad longer.'

'In other words pull my finger out and do something.'

'Yep, it's the only way.'

His brother was right, and about far more than getting his mother on board. Tonight he'd find the courage to talk to Louise properly. She deserved nothing less than his honesty.

13

Louise hesitated at the melodic sound of an acoustic guitar. She'd arranged to meet Josh on the porch but someone else must have laid claim to their planned spot. A deep, raspy voice began to sing heartbreaking lyrics about a man unable to save a friend and watching him die. She eased the door open and discovered Josh sitting in the dark with tears trickling down his face. Taking several deep breaths first she crossed the room and sat down quietly on the floor in front of him. As the song came to an end he rested one hand on her head.

'A musician as well? I shouldn't be surprised but I am. Did you write that yourself?'

'I co-wrote it with a buddy of mine a few years ago.' Josh conceded.

'You always say you can't talk about

your army days but you just did.' She gestured towards the guitar. 'With that song.'

'Yeah. I guess Chad was right.' The ghost of a smile pulled at his mouth.

She waited for Josh to explain his ambiguous statement and after a couple of halting attempts he got it all out. Louise framed a clear picture of a music therapy centre on the unused Robertson land in Leiper's Fork. 'What a fantastic plan. Have you always played?'

'Pretty much. I picked up one of Dad's old guitars as a kid but when he heard me messing around he insisted I had proper lessons and — '

'Being stubborn it put you off.'

'You know me too damn well.' The grouse came along with a tired smile. 'I started writing my own music and I've always hauled one around with me wherever I went.' He tapped on the guitar's well-worn surface. 'This one could tell a few stories. It's travelled as many miles as I have.'

'You'd be ideal to lead the therapy centre.'

'But I'm not a professional musician or a therapist.'

'That doesn't matter. You can hire people to work with you. If other veterans hear the way you've told your personal story through your music it'll help to free up the feelings inside them too.' She gave a sly smile. 'It won't do you any harm either. Help with all that 'opening up' you hate.'

Josh stood the guitar carefully by his chair. 'Sit with me?'

Louise didn't say a word and settled herself on his lap, unable to hold back a contented sigh as he wrapped his arms around her. Strong. Secure.

'How's the rest of your day been?'

'Maggie bullied me into keeping the dress.' She sensed his happy smile against her cheek. 'Did you and Chad get fixed up with your tuxedos?'

'Oh, yeah. I'll be James Bond reincarnated on Saturday.'

The mental image of Josh's dark,

hard masculinity clothed in a smooth exterior made her shiver and it wasn't easy to get her mind back on track. 'I went out with your mother this afternoon and we tracked down a lot of English chocolate for the wedding favour bags. I'd never heard of such a thing before but apparently at most weddings here they give the guests something memorable to take home.'

'If you say so, sweetheart. Cornwall is a beautiful place, right?'

Josh's unrelated question took her by surprise. 'Um, yes, a lot of people say it's the prettiest area in the whole of the country. Why?'

'I'm not sure yet. I've got the beginning of an idea. I'll work on it and show you if it pans out.'

Louise reached up and traced the planes and shadows of Josh's strong, lean face with the tips of her fingers making him grasp her hands and clutch them to his chest. His mouth found hers and he dragged them into a wonderful deep kiss, losing her over and over again. Out of the blue her stomach roiled and the memory of Craig Merton's searching hands slammed back into her. It'd been five years. Would she ever forget?

'I'm sorry. I can't do this.' She struggled to push herself off Josh's lap but he tenderly held her in place.

* * *

'I'm not Craig Merton. I'll never do anything you don't want.' If he got this wrong he'd blow everything apart. 'If I could wipe away what he did to you I would.'

'I hate the hold he still has on me. I want to . . . be with you . . . completely.'

'Give yourself time. I can. All the time you need.' Josh tried to reassure her. 'Trust me you definitely don't have a problem with kissing. In fact if you were any better I'd be a dead man.' A hint of satisfaction pulled at the corners of her lush mouth and Josh stamped down the urge to kiss her again. 'Are you okay with me simply holding you?' She nodded and wriggled into him, resting her head against his shoulder. 'You ready to hear some of my secrets?'

'Only some?'

Josh chuckled. 'All at once might be overkill. I'd prefer you to be still speaking to me in the morning.'

'I'm listening.'

He started to explain how the burden of his father's expectations made him feel as a child growing up. 'We've always clashed. From the time I was old enough to understand he went on and on about the Robertson legacy and that as the oldest son it was my responsibility to take over the business.' Josh managed a half-hearted smile. 'Of course I turned into the stereotypical angry teenage boy. My clothes. My choice of friends. The music I listened to. We argued over everything.' He wished he could stop there but Louise's clear grey eyes kept their steady focus on him. 'Then there was Ellen.' Quietly he told her all about his first love. 'I know we were young and it wouldn't have worked out long-term, but — '

'Your father could've been more subtle but that's not his way.' She hesitated briefly. 'But his heart was in the right place. Good parents try to protect their children and in his mind that's what he was doing. I wish either of mine cared half as much for me.'

'I guess you're right.'

'Maybe one day you'll be able to tell him so?'

'I hope so but I'm not there yet.'

'Give yourself time.' Louise repeated his own words back at him.

'You know it's strange but Ellen's been in the back of my mind all these years and I've often wondered if we could maybe have beaten the odds but when I saw her again . . . it was like bumping into an old friend.' He struggled to explain his lack of any emotional response. 'Maybe there's something wrong with me.'

'Don't be silly.' Louise smiled. 'We all

change. At fifteen my teenage heart crushed over Take That and I stuck posters of Gary Barlow all over my bedroom walls at Jules' house. I know it's not the same but do you understand what I'm getting at?'

'Yeah, I think so.' He received another steady stare and Josh's heart raced. What would she ask of him next?

'Are you ready to talk about your time in the army?'

'I guess.' Not the most enthusiastic response but she wouldn't expect him to jump up and down at the prospect of baring his soul even further.

'What did you enjoy most about the way of life?'

Her unexpected question made him think. 'The sense of a common purpose. I mostly did reconnaissance work which meant we were the first ones into a situation. I relied on the other soldiers in my team and they relied on me. You don't get that level of trust in civilian jobs.'

'And the worst part?'

'Where to start?' Josh exhaled a leaden sigh. 'The children. Traumatised. Heartbroken. Pleading for help because their lives were ripped apart. They fill my mind at night and keep me from sleep. I used to be able to separate myself but the older I got the harder it became.'

'I'm guessing you lost friends?'

'Too many to count.' His voice became bone-dry in his throat. 'They haunt me at night too. You go over incidents time and time again in your head and wonder what you could've done differently to change the outcome.'

'You did your best.'

'Did I? Can you be sure? Can I?'

'Yes, I can. And you should too.' There was nothing of the tentative, scared woman about Louise any longer and Josh's admiration for her grew.

'Do you believe the same about yourself where Merton's concerned?' His pointed question made her shudder in his arms. 'I'm sorry, I — '

'No, you're absolutely right to ask and I'm really trying.'

146

'Yeah, well, I'm doin' the same. Do you want to work on it together?' Josh suggested.

'What exactly are you asking?'

He didn't know how to answer her.

'How about another kiss while you think?'

'Not much thinking will happen then.'

'Would that be so awful?'

Josh slid a hand behind her neck to bring her mouth within kissing distance and her intoxicating perfume surrounded him. 'Louise, I — '

'Should we call it a day for now and just say good night?' Louise gently extricated herself from his arms and stood up. 'Audrey will wonder where I am. I'll see you in the morning.'

She'd completely misunderstood his reticence. 'Don't go.' He sprung up and seized her hands. 'Let's have that kiss. I didn't want to rush you, that's all.'

'I assume it's all right if I rush myself?' A sliver of good humour brightened her eyes. '*I'll* kiss *you* if that makes it easier?' She didn't wait for an answer and he relaxed into her kiss.

Several wonderful minutes later Louise drew away and her face shone with happiness in the glimmer of light filtering onto the porch.

'You shameless woman.' He teased. 'Off with you.'

'Good night.' When she walked away there was a distinct swing in her step and Josh knew he'd put it there.

Thank goodness he had a lot of work to do tonight because he certainly wouldn't sleep.

14

'You'll need to fit your wedding planning duties around lunch out today,' Audrey declared. 'We're all invited to the Pineapple Room at Cheekwood for a small family gathering to meet Mrs Robertson Senior.'

Louise plastered on a smile.

'I'm sure she'll be *most* interested in you.'

She didn't bother to ask why after the grilling she'd received last night. Audrey spotted Louise's pink cheeks and shining eyes when she came upstairs and went into full inquisitor mode. Of course she'd ended up telling the old lady everything.

'You must wear something decent and don't argue with me this time. I'm not convinced Joshua is good enough for you but we're not going to give his grandmother any ammunition to use against you. The fact that he's hardly

149

the last word in smart well-dressed men will be irrelevant to his doting grandmother,' Audrey scoffed. 'I'd suggest the cerise and white floral dress you bought in Exeter.'

'Are there any other instructions?' Louise's arch comment drew out a tight smile from her employer.

'Do your hair up and wear your pearls. Make it perfectly clear you're not a desperate money-grabber.'

'That's hardly an issue. I assume Josh has an army pension but — '

'Oh my dear child, don't be naive. Look around you.' Audrey gestured around the elegant room. 'This house and the contents alone are worth millions. Robertson Guitars is a successful worldwide business going back three generations. The family has large property holdings and don't forget their extensive china and art collections.' Her sharp eyes fixed on Louise. 'Joshua will be a very wealthy man one day if he isn't already. It doesn't change who he is, Louise.'

Doesn't it? She'd worked hard for everything she had and stupidly assumed Josh to be the same.

Audrey scrutinised her. 'Why are you acting as though the world has come to an end? Don't be a reverse snob. I expected better of you. Joshua struck out on his own path as a young man and he's continued to do so. That's extremely admirable.'

Knowing her employer was right didn't soothe Louise's unease. 'I told Tricia I'd help to put the wedding favour bags together this morning. I'd better go.'

'Ask a few subtle questions about Joshua's grandmother while you're there. It might come in handy. Have I also mentioned that we're going out tonight?'

'No. Dare I ask where?'

'We've already seen a lot of the normal tourist venues and I enjoyed the Carter House and the little town of Franklin very much. The Country Music Hall of Fame was surprisingly interesting too.'

'But?'

Audrey's eyes lit up with an air of

151

mischief. 'I keep hearing everyone talk about the honky-tonks on Lower Broadway but I want to see them for myself. It will give me something to shock my friends with when we go back to Cornwall.'

'Oh my God you're serious, aren't you?'

'Of course. Chandler and Maggie are in charge of making the plans and I insist that you and Joshua come too. Tricia's going to babysit little Rose so Emily and Jonathan can have a well-deserved evening out.'

Louise struggled to get her head around the idea of doing a Nashville bar crawl with Audrey in tow. 'I'm sure it'll be a fun evening.'

Audrey wagged her finger. 'At least *try* to appear enthusiastic. I pay you enough.'

'Shall I practice doing a line dance now to get us both in the mood for tonight?'

'Don't be cheeky. Off you go and stuff useless things people don't want into silly bags.'

Louise laughed and walked away without a word.

★   ★   ★

Josh frowned at Ellen's text.

Great to see you looking so good. Do you want to meet and catch up on old times?

'What's up, bro?' Chad strolled in munching on a bagel with one hand and holding onto Maggie with the other.

'What do you pair make of that?' He thrust out his phone and Maggie instantly snatched it, letting Chad read over her shoulder.

'I'm sure her husband wouldn't approve. I wouldn't go if I was you.'

'Don't worry I'm not interested in dragging up the past or getting on the wrong side of Will Harding. He was always handy with his fists in school and I doubt he's changed. I'm not gonna encourage her and reply.'

Chad grinned. 'Crazy isn't it? All you

did was come back to Nashville and the women are crawling out of the woodwork.'

'I'll apologise on behalf of my tactless fiancé.' Maggie shook her head. 'What he really meant was that Louise is a lovely woman and he hopes things work out for you both.'

'Oh yeah I'm sure that's what he meant being the ultimate new man and all that. Changing the subject are we all looking forward to interrogation-by-grandmother?'

'We're good. She thinks Maggie is the best thing since sliced bread,' Chad boasted. 'You're the one who's going to be stretched on the rack.'

'Hey, I've handled far worse and survived.'

'Good luck.' Chad poked at the arm of Josh's crumpled shirt. 'You'd better butter up Betty Lou and get her to wield the iron on that mess.'

'I'm going to change. Satisfied?' Josh groused and left the room with Chad's mocking laughter ringing in his ears.

* * *

He eyed the dainty chairs and wondered if they were strong enough to hold a full grown man. The restaurant's understated decor, botanical prints around the walls and starched white table clothes were aimed at the 'ladies who lunch'. The Nashville social set could catch up on all the local gossip and support the famous gardens and art museum at the same time.

Josh's mother frequently brought him to Cheekwood as a child but normally his father would claim he was too busy to join them. Big J knew she'd drag them around every single plant which was more than he could endure. For a boy the biggest treat was coming in here to the Pineapple Room after he'd trailed after his mother around the gardens and ordering the Tropical Delight sundae. The menu claimed the oversized dessert to be 'ideal for sharing' but he'd never needed any help in demolishing the whole thing.

He fiddled with his tie and ran a hand down over his freshly cut hair.

'They haven't eaten yet so be careful.' Louise's teasing voice by his shoulder took him by surprise. 'And another word of warning. Your grandmother and Audrey are like this already.' She crossed her fingers. 'It took all of five minutes for them to become best friends.'

'Wonderful,' he groaned, 'that's exactly what we don't need.' Josh ran his gaze over her. 'You on the other hand are a sight for sore eyes.'

A tinge of colour lit up her cheeks.

'Beautiful.' He kissed her cheek.

'It's new. Audrey persuaded or rather ordered me to wear it today.'

'Oh, yeah, the dress is beautiful too.' His throwaway comment deepened her blush. 'The colours suit you.' The dark pink and white accentuated her beauty and the nipped waist and full skirt harkened back to the feminine 1950's styles he'd always admired. 'I'm sitting by you.' Louise's silky laughter sent a shot of desire straight through him.

'You'll be lucky. I'm next to your grandmother at one end of the table whereas you are sitting by Audrey at the opposite end. I'm sure they plan to compare notes afterwards.'

'It gets worse,' he groused half-heartedly. 'When we're back at the house I want to show you something.'

Her eyes glittered. 'Why, Mr Joshua, whatever are you talking about? That surely doesn't sound like something a respectable Southern gentleman should ever say to a lady.' Her fake Southern drawl made him burst out laughing and everyone stared at them.

'A real *lady* wouldn't suggest such a thing,' Josh teased before he bent closer to whisper in her ear. 'But to set the record straight I've never claimed to be a gentleman.'

Louise's broad smile assured him that didn't bother her in the least. 'You'd better hurry up and go to see your dear grandmother. Then you can enjoy a dainty quiche and salad lunch and sip on ghastly sweet iced tea.'

'Heathen. You sure don't appreciate the finer things in life.' He purposely deepened his own accent and watched her cheeks burn. 'I'll see you later.' *Time for battle.* Josh made his way towards Audrey and pulled out the empty chair next to her. 'I understand we're lunch companions. How lucky am I?' Her sharp eyes rested on him and Josh squashed the urge to re-check his tie.

'I hope you take advice better than your brother.'

'Would he be getting married on Saturday if he'd listened to you?'

'I was concerned about Maggie. I see now that I was — '

'Wrong?'

'Don't push your luck, young man,' Audrey warned. 'I admit I misread his intentions but I don't regret anything I said at the time.'

A young waitress set down a couple of platters of food in front of them and Josh picked up the nearest one.

'Louise told me about her family and

her trouble with Craig Merton.' Josh offered Audrey the selection of tiny sandwiches. 'I'm sure you can guess what I'd like to do to him. I won't of course because she wouldn't want me to.'

'They always say there's more than one way to skin a cat,' Audrey observed.

'What're you suggesting?'

'I'm not certain yet but I'm far from the only person in the Art Deco collector's world who isn't fond of Mr Merton. He's upset a lot of people with his questionable business tactics. When I get back home I'll make a few enquiries.' She lowered her voice. 'I know his personal troubles with Louise occurred several years ago but it's still affecting the poor girl and I'd like to do something to help. Would you mind if I discuss this with your grandmother? She's a sharp lady and might have any bright ideas. I'll be discreet.'

Josh must've raised his eyebrows because she gave his arm a sharp tap.

'I do know how.'

159

'Go ahead.' Louise might be angry if she discovered Audrey's plan but if there was a way to make Merton pay surely she'd back them up? 'Count me in.' He reached for another plate. 'Would you care for some quiche?'

'Wow, Josh, what a surprise. I'm amazed to see you here.'

He glanced up to meet Ellen's bright smile. On the edge of his awareness he noticed Louise staring in their direction and wished he could wave a magic wand to make his ex disappear.

15

'I assume that's Ellen Harding?' Louise's voice wasn't quite steady. 'Rather obvious, isn't she?' The woman's dyed blonde hair, tight-fitting emerald dress and towering heels were a million miles from subtle. Ellen leaned down towards Josh, low enough to give him an unobstructed view of her generous cleavage.

'She always was,' Rose Ann Robertson scoffed. 'Of course that was a huge part of her appeal. Subtle doesn't appeal to teenage boys.' She gave Louise a sly smile. 'By the way the view over the gardens is spectacular from this room. Maybe you'd care to take a walk over to the windows and admire it?'

Within minutes of meeting Josh's grandmother she'd come to the conclusion the woman was on her side, something she'd have to thank Audrey for later. 'That's a wonderful idea.'

'I'm surprised Joshua didn't offer to take you outside onto the patio for a closer look.'

'How could I have forgotten? I believe he did.' Louise played along. 'If you'll excuse me.' Amateur dramatics was one of her hobbies back in Cornwall and she would treat this as another performance. Smoothing down her dress she ran a hand over her hair and tucked in a rogue strand that'd worked loose.

'Josh, darling.' She flashed a brilliant smile and rested a proprietary hand on his arm. 'I'm dreadfully sorry to interrupt but you promised to show me the view from the patio.' The slight pout she contrived made his mouth curve with amusement. 'Aren't you going to introduce me?'

He sprung to his feet. 'Of course. This is Ellen Harding, an old friend of mine.' He gestured to Ellen. 'This is — '

'Louise Giles.' She stuck out her hand before he could continue. 'I'm delighted to meet you.'

'You must be from England.'

'How ever did you guess?' *Maybe because of the over-exaggerated accent?* She slipped her hand through Josh's arm and gazed at him in blatant admiration.

'I'd better go. The rest of my party are waiting for me to join them,' Ellen murmured.

What a great idea. 'Come along, Josh darling. I'm longing for some fresh air.'

'Sure thing, sweetheart.' Josh turned back to his old girlfriend. 'Take care, Ellen. Enjoy your lunch.' He slipped an arm around Louise's waist and steered her away.

'Oh, wow it really is lovely,' she exclaimed as they stepped outside. The patio's weathered wood, red-tiled floor and wrought iron tables and chairs blended well into the natural surroundings. Josh led her to the far corner of the patio further away from peering eyes and proceeded to give her a long wonderful kiss.

'Thank you for rescuing me or should I be thanking my grandmother?'

'A little of both,' Louise admitted.

'You put the wind up *me* so I'm damn sure it did the trick with Ellen.' He sounded relieved.

'They'll send out a search party if we're gone too long.'

'Yeah.' Josh groaned and pushed away. 'You're driving me crazy. Sorry. It's not your fault. Don't think I — '

Louise gave him a swift, hard kiss on his mouth to shut him up. 'We'll have a quick look at the view and you can tell me something about this place before we go back inside and get through lunch.' She grinned. 'Have you heard we're going to experience the dubious delights of the Nashville honky-tonks tonight?'

'Yeah, Chad passed on that piece of good news. It'll be an experience with Audrey tagging along that's for sure.'

'Hopefully my little exhibition squashed Ellen's dreams of rekindling anything with you.'

'I sure hope so but she was always very determined.' Josh made a grab for Louise's hand. 'Let's forget about her. Come on.' They stood together by the railing and looked out over the lush gardens stretching out in front of them. 'In case anyone asks I'll give you the condensed story of Cheekwood. The Cheek family were wealthy Nashville entrepreneurs back in the late 1800s and bought one hundred acres of land here to build a country estate. The limestone mansion and formal gardens are based on designs from several grand English estates. The Cheek family only ended up living here for about twenty years before they made a gift of it with the condition it was turned into what you see today.' Josh pointed in the distance. 'Maggie and Chad's wedding ceremony will be in the Wills Perennial garden over there and the flowers are at their peak right now. The reception is in one of the mansion's gallery rooms and should be pretty impressive.' Josh sneaked a quick kiss. 'Of course you'll probably compare it to the real thing back home and find it lacking.'

'I'm sure it'll all be beautiful.'

'Not as beautiful as you.' His casual declaration stunned Louise into silence. 'We'd better get back inside before I decide I don't want to share you.'

This man turned her inside out every single time.

★ ★ ★

'Oh, wow, you must've been up all night working on this.' The normally tough ex-soldier flushed with embarrassment and shuffled from one foot to the other. 'What gave you the idea in the first place?' When they all returned to Magnolia House after lunch Josh spirited her off to this media room in the basement. What he'd just shown her blew Louise away.

'You did because you kept saying no one here knows much of anything about where Maggie comes from and that it'd be good to have a mix of the

166

two cultures at the wedding.' His short, snappy explanation betrayed his uneasiness at her attempt to praise him. 'It's no big deal. I threw together a few images of Cornwall and Tennessee and set them to music. People can watch it on a continuous loop at the reception.'

Downplaying his talents and achievements was typical of Josh. His grandmother bragged about him over lunch because he'd received a presidential award for bravery for saving one of his comrades from certain death. Louise was certain she'd never have found that out in a million years from close-mouthed Josh.

'Well I think it's amazing. I assume you wrote the music yourself?'

'Yeah. So what?' He started to fiddle with the projector. 'Every other person in Nashville writes music. It's no big deal.'

She seized his hands which forced him to look at her. 'Yes, it is a big deal and Maggie and Chad will think so too.'

'Do I get a kiss as my reward?'

'How can I resist such a heartfelt plea?'

'You can *always* say no. *Always.*'

'Oh, Josh, I know that.' She wound her arms around his neck. 'Am I making myself perfectly clear now?'

'I guess but how about makin' me absolutely sure?'

'You devil,' she murmured.

'Hey, big brother, I hope I'm not interrupting.' Chad breezed into the room. 'Yep, thought I might be.'

Louise's attempt to break free from Josh's hold failed when he tightened his arms around her waist.

'If this lady wasn't here I'd tell you where to go, baby brother.'

'If she wasn't here it wouldn't matter, would it?' Chad chuckled. 'Roll call in thirty minutes. We're going for dinner at Pinewood Social first before we slum it.' He tapped Louise's arm. 'The Dragon Lady is looking for you. I told her you were working on wedding plans but I'm not sure she believed me. See ya soon.' He strolled away, whistling cheerfully under his breath.

'I'd better go,' Louise murmured.

'Yeah, me too. By the way I'm wearing my old jeans tonight and Audrey will have to put up with it. I'm not gonna look like a tourist in my home town.' His feeble complaint made Louise smile. 'You never let me be a misery, do you?'

'No, because you're not that way inside. It's simply become a habit.'

'You're far too smart.'

Louise pressed a swift, hot kiss on his mouth. 'I'm glad you realise it. Bye.' She ran off before he could stop her and hurried upstairs to pacify Audrey.

★   ★   ★

Josh couldn't remember the last time he enjoyed himself this much. Most of his amusement came from watching Audrey who was taking in every detail of the evening as if she was studying the inhabitants at a zoo.

Pinewood Social was the new hot

spot in town. Josh hadn't been there before but the huge building housed a coffee bar, restaurant, bowling alley, outdoor pool and karaoke bar. Audrey handled the fried pork rinds, catfish, chicken livers and hot chicken they'd insisted she tried with her usual aplomb.

Tootsie's Orchid Lounge was another story.

'Aren't you going to rescue her?' Louise asked.

'Nah, I don't think so.' He grinned. 'She wanted to see the 'real' Nashville and we're givin' it to her.' The large honky-tonk was named for its famous purple-painted exterior and considered one of the top party spots. Audrey had been adopted by a crowd of half-drunk girls on a bachelorette party and he'd overheard them encouraging the old lady to talk so they could listen to her. One of the ringleaders yelled at the top of her voice that they'd found the elderly countess from Downton Abbey. 'Don't fret. I'm keeping an eye on things and so is Chad.' He gestured towards Emily and Jonathan who were busy enjoying the line dancing. 'We're not relying on that pair. They're definitely behaving like typical new parents on the loose for the evening.'

'I suppose she'll be all right.'

'She won't come to any harm. I'm guessin' she'll be tired out after this.'

'Maybe.' Louise shrugged. 'For a woman of seventy-five with severe arthritis she's got incredible stamina.'

He slipped his arms around her waist and pulled her close. The heat from the crowded room and the drift of perfume rising from Louise's warm skin stirred him to say something out of character. 'Chad can take Audrey duty for a while. We're gonna dance.' *Voluntarily dancing? He must be losing it.*

'Don't you normally *ask* women here, or is Nashville different?'

'Heck, lady, cowboys don't ask,' Josh drawled, deepening his accent.

'I noticed you're wearing your boots tonight but where's your ten-gallon hat?' she teased. 'Is your horse tied up outside?'

'He sure is. Ole Gypsy will take us home safely later.'

Her eyebrows arched in amusement. 'So your father's pretty white limousine won't be out there waiting?'

'Damn I don't believe it,' Josh complained, 'she's here again.'

'Who is?'

'Why Josh, and . . . Lucy wasn't it?' Ellen Harding stared artlessly at them both. 'What a coincidence.'

I doubt it very much. 'Isn't it. This is Louise — as I'm sure you remember.'

She giggled and swayed slightly, trailing her long red manicured nails down his arm. 'Don't be like that, Josh darling.'

'I'm not being 'like' anythin'.'

'It's lovely to see you again, *Mrs* Harding.' Josh loved Louise's pointed emphasis on Ellen's marital status. 'I hope you'll excuse us but we were just about to go and dance.'

'Good luck.' Ellen's raucous laughter

made the people around them stare. 'He's always had two left feet.'

'In that case we'll be a good pair because I can't dance to save my life.' Louise gave an ingratiating smile and made a move to push Ellen's hand off his arm but he beat her to it.

'Get your hands off my goddamn wife.'

Josh spotted Ellen's husband pushing through the crowd and quickly shoved Louise back out of the way. Will Harding's raised fists and the dark red anger suffusing his florid face convinced Josh the man planned to fight first and ask questions later. He made a swift grab for Will's arm in mid-air and punched his other fist hard into the man's stomach sending him crumpling to the ground. Out of the corner of his eye he caught sight of Louise's abject horror and took a guess he'd have a whole lot of explaining to do later.

16

'Oh, my God, you've killed him,' Louise shrieked.

'Nah.' Josh's laconic reply earned him a disbelieving glare. 'Self-defence. Chad wouldn't have appreciated his best man turning up with a black eye or a broken nose.'

Ellen crouched on the floor by her husband and glowered at Josh. 'I always knew you were a brute.'

'Oh, Ellie, get real. You think I'm just goin' to stand there and let him slug me?'

'What's up, bro?' Chad touched his shoulder.

'Why don't you take the rest of the gang on home? I need to stay and get this sorted.'

'I'll stay with you,' Louise offered but he sensed her reticence.

'I'll be fine.' Josh kissed her cheek.

'I'll catch up with you later.' A part of Josh hoped that she'd argue with him but she nodded and disappeared to join Audrey.

'We should call the police.' Ellen helped her husband to sit up and tossed Josh another dark look.

'Fine by me.' There were plenty of witnesses to the fact that Will threw the first punch. Josh stood up for himself and those he was responsible for. He refused to alter the core of who he was for anyone.

'Don't be dumb, Ellen.' Will complained. 'I don't need the bad publicity.' There was no concern for his wife only his own reputation. It wouldn't look good for a well-known local businessman to make the news headlines for fighting in a honky-tonk over his wife's alleged interest in another man. 'Help me up.' He grabbed his wife's arm and staggered to his feet. 'You. Outside.' Will pointed at Josh.

'Don't be a moron. We're not two cowboys in a spaghetti Western having a shoot-out over a girl.' He gestured towards an empty table. 'Why don't we sit down, get a drink and talk this through?'

'He doesn't need any more to drink,' Ellen snapped.

A wave of tiredness swept over Josh. Right now he wished himself back in Colorado where the most trouble he ever had came from being a few days overdue on his newspaper bill.

'Get me a beer,' Will barked, 'and she drinks rum and Coke although I'm pretty damn sure you know that.'

The crowd around them thankfully broke up when it became clear the fight was over and Josh quietly fetched the drinks. 'There you are.' He swiftly went on the offensive before Ellen could put her own twist on the story. 'Ellen brought a wedding present over to the house from her parents for Maggie and Chad. We talked for a few minutes and that was it.' Josh hoped Ellen would get the hint that he didn't want to throw her under the bus but needed her help.

'We happened to bump into each other again at Cheekwood yesterday. I was having a pre-wedding lunch with my family and Ellen was there too with a few of her friends.' *Say something. It's your marriage under threat here.*

'He's right, Will. It was Clara's birthday and the girls got together to celebrate, that's all.' The layer of pleading in her voice made Josh nauseous. He never wanted any woman to tiptoe around his sensibilities.

'So what's your damn excuse for being *here*?' Will laid back in on Ellen. 'I heard you talking on the phone to Joe and we both know you rarely speak to your loser of a brother. Then you started calling your girlfriends.'

'You checked my phone?'

'Yeah so what?' Will's hectoring tone put Josh's teeth on edge. 'When y'all agreed to come here it got me wonderin' what you were up to. In the normal way of going along you wouldn't be seen dead in a place like this.'

Ellen threw Josh a panicked look.

'It's not a big deal, Will.' He strove to sound casual. 'I heard that Garth Brooks was singing here tonight and remembered he was an old favourite of Ellen's. I asked Joe to pass the word on in case she was interested.' Until Joe Carter turned up to drive their limousine tonight Josh hadn't even realised his father still employed Ellen's older brother but Will Harding didn't need to find out that piece of information.

'Garth Brooks? I don't remember seeing his name up outside.'

'Yeah well, it got cancelled. He's sick.' If Will checked on his story they'd be screwed. 'You've got nothing to worry about, pal. Ellen's a one man woman and I'm hopin' to get hitched myself soon.' A wild exaggeration but he couldn't take it back now. 'I need to get goin'. Hope I didn't do any damage.'

'Nothing serious.' Will cracked a smile. 'You've got quite a punch on you.' He gave Ellen a weary glance. 'Come on, let's get you home.'

'Thanks, Josh, take care of yourself.' Ellen's quiet words were accompanied by a grateful smile.

If nothing else he'd laid that side of his past well and truly to rest. In an odd way Ellen did him a favour but getting Louise to agree was the next challenge.

★   ★   ★

Louise ignored Audrey's pointed stares and heavy sighs all the way back to Magnolia House. 'If you don't need me for anything else I fancy an early night. It's been a long day.'

'I'll be perfectly fine. Rose Ann asked me to stop in to see her when we got back. She wants to hear *all* about the evening.'

I'm sure you'll enjoy giving her every gruesome detail including the part where her grandson thumped the husband of his ex-girlfriend. And when I left without staying to help him. 'I'm going down to make a cup of tea. Would you care for some?'

'No, thank you, dear. I believe there's a particularly fine brandy on my horizon to round off an eventful evening.'

Louise's cheeks burned. 'Good night.' She hurried away before Audrey could start on her again.

'The kettle's boiled. I hoped you might head this way.' Josh's laconic voice startled her the moment she stepped into the kitchen.

'Oh. What are you doing here?'

He raked her with his amused gaze. 'I live here. Did you forget?'

How could I?

'You'll be relieved to hear the police didn't get involved and Will Harding walked out of Tootsie's under his own steam with his adoring wife on his arm.' He dangled a tea bag in front of her face. 'Do you need this?'

'No thank you. We brought our own loose tea from England because Audrey won't drink anything else.' Being within touching distance of Josh the teasing hint of his familiar plain soap in the air affected her deeply. Everything about him was straightforward from his simple black T-shirt and sexy ripped jeans to his thick, short-cropped dark hair, given a bluish sheen by the florescent light. A woman got exactly what she saw with Josh.

'I'm sorry, Louise.' He opened his arms wide, cocking his head to one side with a quirky smile. 'Am I forgiven?'

'For what?'

'Scaring you.'

'I was afraid,' she whispered and dropped her gaze away. 'I know you're tough and can defend yourself but I thought you'd badly hurt Ellen's husband.' Louise tripped over her words. 'If the police took you away and I went back to England without seeing you again you'd never know . . . ' She dissolved into tears.

'Don't cry.' Josh wrapped his arms around her in a tight bear hug, his voice breaking. 'The toughness is only on the outside. I can't stand it when anyone I love is hurtin'.' Louise stared at him in shock.

'Don't freak out. I know what I said and I meant it but I was a complete mess when my cat got run over. I was only five and — '

'Your cat?'

A whoosh of heat lit up his face. 'Yeah, I mean I loved Daisy and . . . she turned out to be okay but there's different sorts of love and — '

'Stop there.' She held up her hand. 'You're digging a deeper hole.'

'Story of my life,' Josh muttered half under his breath.

'I'm going to bed. I need time to think about . . . all this.' A mixture of natural caution and uncertainty held Louise back. While she still had an ounce of self-discipline left Louise walked away and hurried upstairs. She took refuge in her bedroom and struggled to catch her breath. *You know Josh is different. He's plain-spoken and truthful.* But how could she be certain?

17

Josh's jaw ached with the effort to keep smiling. It hadn't been difficult to stay out of Louise's way all morning now all he had to do was survive the late afternoon rehearsal and the family dinner afterwards.

I need time to think about . . . all this.

After tomorrow's wedding he'd give her all the time in the world by getting into his rusty truck and clearing off back to Colorado.

He hadn't expected Louise to declare her undying love for him but her apparent rejection sliced Josh to the bone. Forty years old and in love for the first time. The romance gods were having a field day.

'Hey, big brother, Maggie needs your help with our wedding cake.' Chad strolled into the family room. 'She won't let me in there because for some dumb reason I'm not allowed to see it until tomorrow.'

'Sure.' Josh dragged himself off the sofa. 'Is she in the kitchen?'

'Yep.' Chad frowned. 'What's up with you?'

'Nothing.'

'Liar. Spit it out. Every time you think no one's looking you go back to your old grouchy self. Louise is trailing around with a long face and sad eyes. Don't tell me you screwed up again?'

'Why assume it's my fault?' he retorted. 'I told the damn woman I loved her. All right? But she ran off so fast you'd think her tail was on fire. Are you satisfied now?' Josh glowered.

'Are you sure you didn't misunderstand?' Chad ventured. 'Maybe she needed more time.'

'Yeah, yeah I got that old chestnut. We both know that's gal talk for 'not in a million years'. Seems pretty clear from where I'm standing.'

'Maybe you just took her by surprise.'

Josh scoffed. 'Yeah, right, I'm sure. You carry on believing that. I'm headin' back to Colorado when the confetti settles.'

'What about your plan for the therapy centre?'

'Get real. It's a damn fool notion like my stupid idea of falling in love and leading a normal life.' He hated the sympathy oozing from his brother. 'Quit it, Chad. I'm off to help your lovely bride now. You've got a good one there. I'm pleased one of us lucked out. You deserve it.' He added the last part automatically although he'd seen enough suffering in his time in the military to know 'deserving' had little to do with the direction of anyone's life.

★ ★ ★

'We don't need any more people cluttering up the place.' Louise's firm tone stopped Josh in the doorway. 'Maggie's asked me to help her with the wedding cake.'

185

'Really? Chad sent me here for the same reason.' Josh's laconic drawl made her hot all over. 'Where is the lady in question anyway?'

'I'm not sure. On her way I suppose.'

'I'm guessin' we've been had.'

The brief flash of amusement in his gold-sparked eyes irked her until the penny dropped. 'I spotted Audrey and your grandmother in close conversation after breakfast.'

'Damn. Tell me you didn't blab about — '

'Of course I didn't mention our . . . whatever you want to call it last night,' she mumbled.

'You should know by now those two devious women don't need written proof.' Josh's warm laughter filled the room. 'They're perfectly capable of adding two and two together and coming up with whatever total suits them best.'

'I've got better things to do than humour them even if you haven't.'

'Like what?'

Anything that takes me out of your

reach. I can't put a sensible thought together while you stand there looking heart-stoppingly gorgeous and smelling delicious and . . .

'Louise. You're killin' me all over again. I know you asked for time but . . . '

His voice trailed away and she ached to kiss away the deep lines creasing his face.

'If I'm barking up the wrong tree tell me and I'll leave you alone. Maybe it was too soon.' He shrugged. 'But I know deep down you feel something for me.'

'It isn't hard to be attracted to a good-looking man who's obviously interested in you.' Louise fought to hold onto the protective wall she'd built around her heart.

'Really. So any man could do this?' Before she could protest he grasped her shoulders and brought his mouth down hard on hers. His kiss swept through her like a wildfire and pooled at the pit of her stomach. 'Does that prove my point?' Josh flashed a triumphant smile.

'By forcing yourself on me?' As soon as the words left her mouth Louise wished them unsaid. 'Oh, Josh, I never meant — '

'Don't you dare tar me with the same brush as Craig Merton.' His stony expression broke her heart.

She jerked from his grasp and ran across the room, fumbling uselessly with the doorknob in her effort to get out.

'Running away again? It's not the solution.'

'But I don't know how to do this.' Louise rested her head against the door and a sob caught in her throat.

'Nor do I, sweetheart, nor do I.'

His honesty touched a cold place deep inside her and she inched around to face him. 'What're we going to do?' she pleaded.

'I'm not sure. Do you want to work it out together?' Josh came closer to wrap his arms around her and his breath warmed her cheek. 'I promise not to mention a particular four letter word again.'

'What if I *want* you to at some point?'

'Then you'll have to say it first.' There was nothing unkind in his simple statement but he meant every word.

'Fair enough.'

'We'd better go and find our elusive bride.'

'I'm here.' Maggie's impish face poked around the door. 'Are you two friends again?'

'Yes, we are, you meddling — '

'Hush or I'll wash your mouth out with soap,' she teased. 'It worked, didn't it?'

'I guess.' Josh grudgingly admitted.

Louise gave her friend a massive hug. 'I'll say thank you, even if he won't.'

'Did you ever need any genuine cake assistance?' His pointed question made Maggie blush.

'Yes, but not until tomorrow. I will need your help moving it safely to Cheekwood.'

'Is it an English tradition that it's unlucky for the groom to see the cake before the wedding?'

'No, not at all.' Maggie laughed. 'This is simply me. I really want to surprise Chad because I've recreated the cake that met a sad end at the wedding we first met at.'

'Isn't that tempting fate?' Louise asked.

'I hope you've got a couple hundred glass jars ready to stuff the broken pieces in,' Josh joined in.

'You are so not funny.' Maggie glared.

'I think we make a pretty damn good comedy duo.'

'Go away and annoy someone else. How about making sure your brother's got his speech ready?'

'Sure.'

'I assume you've written yours?'

'Yep. All done.'

Louise recognised a lie when she heard one but Maggie's benign smile suggested she'd been suitably fooled. 'Come on, we've got work to do.' She grabbed Josh's hand and practically dragged him from the kitchen. As soon as they were far enough away where they wouldn't be overheard she stood still. 'You haven't written a single word yet have you?'

'Can't I get away with anythin' around you?'

'No and don't be stupid enough to try again.'

'No, ma'am, I won't.' He leaned in and nuzzled her neck. 'Maggie is busy with her cake. Chad's in town getting a haircut. Everyone else is out of the house.'

'And your point is?' Louise struggled to concentrate as he stroked a hand teasingly down her back.

'A few more kisses might inspire me to amazin' literary heights.'

Her awareness centred on his hot, sure hands lingering where they shouldn't.

'The library on the second floor is real quiet.' Josh's wicked grin unravelled her. 'There's a comfortable sofa there too.' Out of the blue a shadow darkened his gleaming eyes. 'I didn't mean . . .'

'I know you didn't.'

'Hey, if I'm ever lucky enough to convince you to go to bed with me it won't be under this roof.' Josh groaned. 'Heck, I'm terrible at this whole seduction business. I should've asked my baby brother for advice.'

'You're brilliant. Trust me. Take me to the library and kiss a speech out of me.'

'That's a deal.'

Louise stamped on her doubts. Could they really make this work? They only had a couple more days together and everyone knew long-distance relationships rarely lasted. She'd read enough self-help books over the years to convince her that, perhaps due to her unstable upbringing, she had a habit of making bad judgments when it came to forming relationships.

'You're thinking too much again.'

'But — '

'If it helps to ease your mind I'm not rushing off right away after the wedding dust settles.'

'Ah, but remember I am.'

'Maybe. Maybe not. Don't jump to conclusions.' A cat-got-the-cream smile slid across Josh's face.

'I've got a return plane ticket with Monday's date on it.'

He tapped the side of his nose. 'Wait and see.' Before she could protest he kissed her again. 'Trust me.'

Perhaps Josh could work a miracle. He wasn't doing badly so far.

18

Josh couldn't wrap his head around why Chad remained affable and calm in the middle of all the wedding eve chaos until he spotted his brother meet Maggie's gaze and watched the two of them smile in unison. After a few pre-wedding wobbles they'd worked out what was important and flowers being the precise shade of yellow didn't make the list. Josh still considered an elopement would solve everything.

'Stop tugging at that tie or your mama will swat you,' Big J hissed in Josh's ear.

'I suggested casual dress for the rehearsal but you'd think I'd asked them to parade around in their underwear,' Josh grouched. 'It's not enough we've gotta be stuffed into a suit and tie all day tomorrow.'

He dabbed at the sheen of sweat on

his face with the clean handkerchief Betty Lou had pressed into his hand on the way out of the door.

'For a forty-year-old man you sure don't know much about women.' His father shook his head. 'Most of 'em like nothing better than dressing up. A wise man smiles, agrees and does what he's told.' He gave a wry smile. 'None of which you're great at. Probably why you're still single.'

Rub it in why don't you? Josh noticed the event supervisor bearing down on them. 'I think we're on.' Maggie and Chad both insisted they didn't want the large wedding party popular in the south with its multiple bridesmaids and matching number of groomsmen. They were sticking with only Josh as the best man and Emily as Maggie's matron of honour.

An unreadable expression settled on his father's face. 'You're doin' a bang-up job. It means a lot to Chad.' Big J fiddled with his shirt cuffs. 'And to me and your mother.'

'I'm trying my best.' Josh exhaled a sigh. 'I always have. I never purposely set out to upset y'all.'

'I know, son.'

He needed to get something out and took a chance that this was as good a time as any. 'I totally get now why you broke Ellen and me up.' Josh cracked a smile. 'Doesn't mean I like the bullying way you went about it but you were trying to protect me from making a dumb, teenage mistake and screwing up my life and hers.'

'Thanks.' Big J grasped his shoulder. 'It means a lot to hear you say that.'

Josh struggled to control his emotions.

'I shouldn't have pushed you all the darn time either about all the other crap. If I'd been more reasonable you might've come into the business.'

'Probably not,' he admitted. 'Even though I love music it's not my thing.'

'If you have your own kids one day you'll find out the first born is kind of a practise run.' Big J cracked a smile.

'You got the short end of the stick.'

'Louise helped me to see you did everything out of . . . love.' Josh stared down at his feet. 'She didn't have that with her folks. Her father's never been on the scene and her mom abandoned her with a half-sister when Louise was fourteen. I see now how damn lucky I've been.'

'I'm the lucky one. It's a miracle you're still talking to me.' His father shoved his hands in his pockets and glared. 'You'd better get on and do your duty and let the women manage the crying for both of us. Chad couldn't have a finer best man.'

His father's gruff tone didn't fool Josh for a minute but he simply gave a brief nod before hurrying away.

The fifteen-minute ceremony took the best part of an hour to rehearse and when they finally got it right they were dismissed with strict instructions to be on time the next day.

'You're good at taking orders. No wonder you got on so well in the army.'

Louise appeared by his side, linking her arm with his. Normally non-family guests wouldn't attend the rehearsal but Audrey insisted on coming, partly because American wedding traditions were so different and she didn't want to make a fool of herself but mostly because she hated to miss out on anything.

'Blue. My favourite colour.' Josh ran his finger under the shoulder strap of her simple linen dress to stroke Louise's bare warm skin.

'I'm guessing tomorrow that will shift to dark red?'

'Oh, yeah, no doubt.' He shifted his other arm around her waist and eased her closer. 'After the rehearsal dinner I want to take you for a drive.'

'Audrey might need me.'

'Persuade her it's in the service of furthering cross-cultural relations.' A flush of heat tinged Louise's cheeks. 'I sure am glad the happy couple decided on a simple barbecue tonight rather than the fancy dinner my folks wanted to host because we can sneak away earlier. Plus I can get rid of this noose.' He tugged at his tie.

'Am I allowed to dress down too?'

'Nope.' He chuckled. 'I'm too fond of this dress. Unless you're gonna swap it for some Daisy Dukes in which case count me in.' By Louise's puzzled expression she didn't have a clue what he was talking about. 'I guess you aren't a fan of the old *Dukes of Hazzard* television show?'

'I've never heard of it, or them, whatever they are.'

'Heck, woman, you've never lived,' Josh teased. 'Google it when we get back to the house.' He grabbed her hand. 'Time to watch Aunt Audrey gnaw on some ribs. That should be good for a laugh.'

* * *

Louise couldn't remember ever being this happy. With a couple of fresh drinks in her hands she stopped to watch Josh from across the garden. He lay sprawled on the grass swinging an empty beer bottle from his fingers and joking with his father.

'You've done wonders for him, hon.' Tricia appeared by her elbow. 'It sure is a blessing.'

'He's a very special man.'

'Yes, he is and I've waited a long time for the right woman to come to the same conclusion. Never thought I'd have to drag one four thousand miles, but hey, whatever it takes.'

'You wouldn't, um, mind if — '

'No, my dear, I wouldn't mind in the least.' Tricia's straightforward answer made Louise smile. 'It's early days but Rose Ann and Audrey are one hundred percent behind you both which means you won't get much choice,' she joked.

Louise's smile wobbled.

'Don't freak out. Nobody's forcing you into anything least of all my Josh. He's not made that way,' Tricia observed. 'But he's always been a boy to know what he wants. Give him a chance and give yourself one too.'

'I want to,' Louise murmured. 'Honestly. I do.'

'Why don't you run along? He said the two of you have plans for the rest of the evening and we'll be wrapping up soon. Our bride needs her beauty sleep.'

'Thank you. I really appreciate your candour.'

'And vice versa.'

Louise nodded and hurried across the lawn to Josh. 'Another beer, oh Lord and Master.'

'Well trained already.' His eyes darkened. 'Are you ready to leave? I need you to myself.'

Her breath caught in her throat. Josh never dressed things up in fancy words and the realisation was incredibly freeing.

'Give me five minutes. Oh by the way I did what you asked.' She kept her voice neutral. 'Catherine Bach certainly had amazing legs, didn't she? Maybe one day you'll get lucky.' Louise watched his jaw slacken before she strolled away.

In the sanctuary of her bedroom she freshened up her lipstick and unpinned her hair, shaking it loose around her shoulders. Exactly five minutes later a sharp knock on the door made her smile. Josh didn't know the meaning of the word late.

'Are you ready?'

'Is someone impatient?' Louise opened the door and Josh's hot grin warmed every inch of her.

'We're gonna have us a real good evening.'

'Are you sure we ought to go out? There must be last minute jobs we should be helping with and Maggie might — '

'We deserve a break and there are plenty of people around if anythin' needs to be done.' Josh hugged her. 'Plus I've a special treat for you. For us both really.'

'Where are — '

'Don't ask. We're goin' to a revered Nashville institution and you'll love it.'

He squeezed her waist. 'Come on. My truck is at your disposal.'

'Please tell me it's not another honky-tonk?'

'You're a lost cause.' Josh shook his head in fake sadness. 'Come on or we'll be late.'

'Is your middle name Stubborn?'

'Nope. It's Claiborne. Bit of a mouthful but it's an old family name.'

'There's a lot we don't know about each other really, isn't there?' she mused and his tawny eyes darkened.

'Does my middle name change how you feel about me?' Under his focused gaze she couldn't lie.

'No, of course not.'

'Good. If it helps my case I'll tell you my oldest childhood memories, every detail of my school years, my favourite foods, movie likes and dislikes and about the first time I kissed a girl and got the braces on our teeth tangled together. Any damn thing you want to know.' Josh's late day stubble brushed against her cheek and stirred her all over again. 'Put all that in proportion. Please.'

Although she wasn't yet a hundred percent convinced Louise refused to spoil the evening. 'You're right. Let's go and enjoy ourselves.'

★   ★   ★

Josh watched her face light up as they stopped in the small car park outside the Bluebird Cafe. 'I remembered you saying you love the *Nashville* TV programme and thought you'd enjoy seeing where they set some of the shows. An old friend of mine is playing tonight and he sent me a couple of tickets.'

'It's not as large as I expected.' Louise glanced at the small shops on either side of the cafe. 'It's not exactly in the centre of things is it?'

'Nope.' He hopped out and ran around to open her door. 'We're five miles outside of downtown Nashville but the Bluebird's been in business going on thirty-three years so I guess they're doing somethin' right.'

'This is so exciting.'

Josh fought down his misgivings and struggled to smile.

'What's wrong? Is this musician someone from your days in the army?'

'Yeah.' He choked out his reply. The last time he'd seen T. Ray Johnson his old friend was being stretchered onto a medevac helicopter, covered in blood and not expected to survive. 'I should've told you the whole story before we came but I didn't think it would be this . . . hard.'

Louise pushed open the door and grabbed his hand. 'Maybe you should have warned me, but now you can buy me a drink and explain everything.'

Josh sensed a challenge behind her simple statement and hoped he'd rise to her expectations. If he couldn't lay out all his fears and nightmares in plain sight and prove himself worthy of being more than a brief encounter in both their lives he didn't deserve her.

19

'I suppose you've been here before.' Louise gazed around the crowded room, bigger than it appeared from the outside but still compact. The first show was over and they'd started to let people in for the late performance.

'Yeah, I grew up coming here. My folks are long-time friends of Amy Kurland who started this place.'

'Have you ever performed?'

Josh grinned. 'You've gotta be kiddin' me. I'm not in this league. Everyone who plays guitar and writes songs would kill to sing here.'

'Tell me about your friend.' Louise ached when he couldn't quite meet her gaze.

'I met T. Ray in training and we hit it off right away. He's from a small town in Alabama. Sharp guy. The type you'd trust your life to. We ended up in the same unit and saw a lot of . . . bad stuff together.' Josh knocked back his beer. 'Fancy another?'

'No thanks. I've barely touched this one. You go ahead if you want.'

He slumped back in the chair. 'I'll wait.'

'Did T. Ray leave the army to pursue a music career?'

'Sort of.' Josh exhaled a heavy sigh. 'Hell, I can't do this now. I've got to . . . see him first. Let's try to enjoy the show and we'll talk after.'

She searched for a different thread of conversation to ease the deep strain etched into his grim features. 'Why don't you tell me a bit more about this place?' Thankfully that did the trick and he launched into the history of the cafe and how it'd become *the* place for Nashville songwriters to showcase their talents. A number of well-known country singers had got their big break here and more than a few record deals were signed in this small room.

'Tonight is one of their 'In the

Round' nights. Three or four songwriters sit in a circle in the middle of the room and take turns playing both separately and together. They chat to each other and the audience. It's cool.'

She loved his enthusiasm but as a round of applause greeted the musicians coming into the room Josh's smile faded and his grip on her hand tightened. Louise instantly guessed which man T. Ray Johnson was. The big-boned, ebony-skinned man carried himself with the same innate confidence as Josh except for his uneven, rolling gait. A flash of relief crossed his face when he eased onto one of the tall stools. The movement caused his jeans to hitch up and she caught a glimpse of metal where his lower legs should be.

Louise said nothing and fixed her attention on the stage. They started by all playing together one of her long time favourites, the Johnny Cash classic 'Ring of Fire' but her heart flipped as T. Ray struck out on his own with the first chord of another familiar song. The searing lyrics soon hushed the audience and reduced many to tears. Josh wiped his eyes and stared at the table.

'Glad to hear y'all loved that one. I co-wrote it with an old pal of mine who's here tonight.' T. Ray pointed to Josh and a spotlight hit him in the face. 'We went through a heck of a lot of rough times, buddy, but we're here and it's all good.'

'How can he fuckin' say that?' Josh hissed. 'He lost his damned legs and told me he wished I'd let him die.'

Louise touched his face. 'Look at him now. Really look at him.' She tilted Josh's head towards the stage. 'I see an incredibly talented man doing something he absolutely loves.'

'Come over and sing with us, Josh,' T. Ray yelled. 'You don't mind, do you guys?' The other musicians shook their heads and shouted their encouragement but Josh didn't move.

'Are you seriously turning down the chance to sing at the Bluebird? I don't believe it and your family won't either.'

'You wouldn't tell them,' he protested.

'Try me.'

'You're a bully.' Josh growled and pushed back his chair.

★ ★ ★

Afterwards he'd struggle to recall this moment but right now every second was crystal clear.

'You know which one we're gonna do.' T. Ray flashed his inimitable grin and shoved a guitar in Josh's hands. 'After the set we'll have a drink together and you can introduce me to your little lady.'

He hadn't sung the classic Lynyrd Skynyrd song 'Sweet Home Alabama' since the day of T. Ray's accident. His friend pleaded to hear it while they waited for the medevac helicopter to arrive certain he'd never see his home state again.

Somehow they got through the song helped by the enthusiastic crowd joining in and stamping their feet.

'I'll let you go now but no runnin' off and hiding again for two years,' T. Ray chided. 'I'm damn glad you came tonight. When I sent the tickets I didn't expect you to turn up.'

'Me neither but I'm glad I did,' Josh confessed. Back at Louise's side he hugged her and fought to get his emotions back under control, absurdly grateful when she didn't say a word.

When the show finished they waited for T. Ray to talk to some of the audience members who'd enjoyed his music. Josh couldn't believe it when one of the show organisers made a point of seeking him out to say how much he enjoyed his music and promised to get in touch about returning to perform another night.

'Are you good to go out for coffee?' T. Ray wandered across to join them. 'I want to share a few stories with this lovely lady.'

'She might run off and leave me if you blab too much.'

'We'd love to, Mr Johnson.' Louise smiled. 'I can't wait to hear your interesting tales about this renegade.'

'Mr Johnson is my daddy.' His raucous laugh reverberated around the room. 'You're best off calling me T. Ray like everyone else.'

'There's a late night doughnut shop a few minutes up the road,' Josh suggested.

'I'll follow you in my truck.' T. Ray patted his stomach. 'Me and sugar have a real close relationship.'

'Me and this sugar do too.' Louise's fierce blush made both men chuckle.

Ten minutes later the three of them were squeezed into the last empty booth and the waitress set down steaming mugs of strong coffee and a plate of fresh doughnuts. For a while they swapped the usual talk of people who hadn't seen each other for a while but one question burned a hole in Josh's brain.

'I've gotta ask you something and you've got to be honest with me, T. Ray.'

212

'Always have been.'

'Do you still wish I hadn't . . . ' The words stuck in his throat.

'Saved me?' T. Ray glanced at Louise. 'Did he tell you what happened?'

'No and please don't feel you have to.'

'I believe I do, ma'am.' T. Ray launched into an eerily calm explanation of the horrific explosion and its aftermath. 'This one dragged me to safety, did first aid and stayed with me 'til the medics came. I wouldn't have survived else.' He tapped Josh's arm. 'I wasn't grateful at the time but I sure am now.'

'Really?'

'Yeah, really, you idiot.' He tapped his prosthetic legs. 'Sure I miss these but hey, I'm alive, I'm doing what I love and I got me a real good woman too.' T. Ray pulled out his wallet and retrieved a picture. 'That's my Peggy. We're getting hitched in September.' His dark eyes focused on Josh. 'I told her there's only one best man on my list. Are you up for the job?'

'Sure. If you want.'

'Nah, I asked because I don't want you, dumbass,' T. Ray joked. 'I'd better be going. Got to head downtown to my hotel. You'd better not disappear off the face of the planet again.'

'I won't.'

They all stood up and headed outside.

'You take good care of this guy. He's the best.' Josh smiled when T. Ray treated Louise to an exuberant hug. 'You make sure you come along with him to my wedding. We'll show you some real down home southern hospitality. None of this fancy Nashville stuff.' His smile turned reflective. 'I'm gonna hug you too pal whether you like it or not.' T. Ray wrapped his beefy arms around Josh and squeezed. 'That didn't kill you, did it?'

'Almost. You might've cracked a couple of ribs. I'll be at the wedding.' He blushed. 'I mean we will. At least I hope so.' Josh tripped over his words. 'I promise.'

'Good, 'cause I know you never break those. We swore to watch each other's backs and you did it to the max. Could've got yourself killed in the process but you never left me for a second.' T. Ray choked up. 'That's enough soul-baring for one night. See ya, kids.' He hurried over to his truck and left them standing and looking at each other.

'Are you ready to go home?' Josh asked. 'It'll be a long day tomorrow.'

'Good idea. I'm tired.'

In the truck Josh rested his hands on the steering wheel for a moment. 'T. Ray would be ideal for my project, wouldn't he?'

'Perfect.'

'Seeing what music's done for him helped cement my decision tonight.' He tweaked her nose. 'You were right. Again.'

'I might need to record that so I can replay it when you're being obtuse.'

'Me? Obtuse?' Josh smothered her face with a shower of kisses. 'You must be confusing me with some other guy.'

'There's no mixing you up with anyone else. Ever,' Louise declared in her usual crisp fashion. 'Take me home, cowboy.' Her soft laughter filled the truck. 'Isn't there a song about cowboys and country roads?'

'Sure is. It's a John Denver classic. I'll sing it to you one day.'

'Good,' Louise murmured and her head lolled on his shoulder as tiredness overtook her. He started up the truck, put it into gear and inched into the deserted road. *You never left me for a second.* He'd kept his promise to T. Ray and in the dark silence Josh made a similar one to the woman sleeping by his side.

20

Maggie glared at them both. 'If you drop that cake I'll never talk to you again.'

Louise swallowed her laughter and didn't dare look at Josh. He'd be thinking on the same lines — in other words — what a relief that would be. They hadn't had a free minute all morning and her only saving grace was the amazing man choking down his own laughter next to her.

'It's not a problem, Maggie.' His silky voice soothed their bride-to-be and her fierce expression softened. 'Go fix yourself a cup of tea. We'll tell you when the cake is safely in place at the art museum. I'll even send pictures to prove it to you.'

'Are you sure? You don't — '

'We've got everything written down.' Josh waved the detailed instructions in

Maggie's face. 'And my trusty assistant is great at taking orders.'

'I must admit I could do with a cup,' Maggie confessed. 'I've got lots more to do before the hairdresser comes at noon and goodness only knows what she's going to do with this appalling mess.' She sighed and tugged at her unruly curls.

'You'll be a beautiful bride,' Louise tried to reassure her. 'Remember Chad loves every inch of you exactly as you are.'

'You're right.' Her eyes welled up with big fat tears. 'I promised him last night that I'd enjoy the day. You've both been incredible and I wouldn't have got through this without you.'

'We've been happy to help,' Josh said. 'You run along and get that tea.' He smiled and shooed Maggie out of the kitchen. 'Heck, if that's what an even-tempered, calm woman gets like over a wedding I wouldn't want to see a real . . . what do you call them?'

'Bridezilla. As in Godzilla but with a

white dress and veil.' Louise giggled. 'Have you got the video organised?'

'Yep, I was there at six this morning setting it up.'

'Didn't you get any sleep?' It'd been after one o'clock before they reluctantly went to their separate bedrooms. 'Too much thinking?'

'Probably. Never a good thing.' His quip emerged without an accompanying smile. 'I kept going over it all. T. Ray. The project. Everything raced around in circles.'

She slipped her arms around his waist and snuggled into his broad chest. No doubt he'd look amazingly hot in a tuxedo later but she loved him most in frayed jeans, an old T-shirt, his work boots and in need of a shave.

'Push all that to one side for today. Chad encouraged Maggie to enjoy the day and you ought to as well.'

'So should you. You didn't come here to organise a wedding.'

'There are a lot of things I didn't come here to do,' she murmured.

'Oh, yeah, and what might they be?'

Louise struggled to think straight as he dragged tantalising kisses all the way down her neck. *Fall in love with you.* Josh's eyes widened. 'Did I just say that out loud?'

'You sure did. I'm guessing you didn't mean to, but — '

'Oh, but I did mean it.' Louise touched her hand to her mouth. 'Goodness.'

'All this wedding hoopla is going to your head.' His voice wobbled. 'You'll be back down to earth tomorrow.'

'I hope not,' she whispered.

'Me too.' Josh cupped his hand behind her neck and drowned them in a long, hot kiss before reluctantly pulling away. 'Cake.'

'Cake.' Louise repeated after him. 'You give the orders and I'll obey. For now at least.'

'You've got a deal.'

★ ★ ★

'Let *me* do your cufflinks. Your damn hands are shaking,' Josh chided his brother. 'You'll never catch me going through all this.'

'Not even if the gorgeous Louise wants a big do?'

'Louise?' Josh croaked. 'We're not talkin' weddings any time soon.'

'I wasn't either when I met Maggie and look at me now.'

Yeah, I am, and I'm envious but it still doesn't mean I'm in a hurry to copy you.

'We'd better get outside for photos before Miss Kathy hassles us again with her timetable and clipboard.' Josh poured out two generous shots of aged Tennessee whiskey. 'Be happy.' They knocked back their drinks in silence.

It didn't take long because there was no large wedding party to work around plus Maggie put her foot down and refused to do any of the bride and groom shots before the ceremony. Most formal American weddings took those early to save time but she insisted it would be bad luck for Chad to see her until she walked down the aisle.

'It's time to get going, bro,' Josh said.

They were supposed to make their way to the Wills Perennial Garden and stand in their assigned spots on the limestone terrace ten minutes before Maggie arrived. The sun clung onto the last remnants of the day casting welcome shadows over the lawn and setting off the lush landscaping, a mass of colourful late spring perennials. The dark wooden chairs were decorated with miniature Cornish and American flags and wide bows of gleaming gold ribbons. As he and Chad walked down the aisle Josh scanned the crowd for Louise. When he caught her eye and winked it earned him a stern look from Audrey.

'Maggie informed me in English weddings the groom doesn't watch the bride coming down the aisle but that's one custom *I* told *her* we weren't adopting. I'm not waiting any longer,' Chad complained. 'Being banished to my condo last night didn't sit well I can tell you.'

'A whole twenty hours apart — don't know how you coped.' Josh's laconic comment earned him a glare. 'After this she's all yours. For life.'

'Damn right.' A broad smile split Chad's face in half. 'There she is.'

The first notes of Handel's 'Water Music' drifted across the lawn.

'Beautiful. So damn beautiful,' Chad whispered. The two women walked arm in arm towards them because Emily was standing in for their late father and giving her younger sister away.

Josh checked his pocket for about the five thousandth time and curled his fingers around the two rings then fumbled in his other pocket to make sure his speech hadn't disappeared. Louise laughed when he admitted he'd rather face down the Taliban unarmed than stand in front of two hundred people and be witty and heartfelt.

'We are here today to celebrate . . . '

The minister's voice brought him

back to the moment and he concentrated, not wanting to miss his cue for producing the rings. Fifteen minutes later Josh gave thanks for the fact Maggie hadn't insisted on an English wedding ceremony which he'd heard could last for a whole hour. He offered his arm to Emily, looking pretty in something he'd call light purple but no doubt had a fancier name, and they followed the new Mr and Mrs Chandler Robertson down the aisle.

'I need a handsome young man to escort me.' His grandmother nabbed him. 'I understand we're taking pictures outside the museum.'

'Sorry, Grammy, but you'll have to make do with me,' Josh teased. 'Your young, handsome grandson is otherwise engaged today, or I should say married.'

Rose Ann tapped his arm with the ornate fan she carried to match her exotic peacock-blue dress. At eighty she still carried herself with the grace and confidence of a young woman. 'If it wouldn't make your head swell I'd repeat the comments I overheard from the women sitting around me during the ceremony. You've acquired quite a fan club.'

'They all need eye-tests,' he quipped.

'Your mama put a flea in Audrey's ear and convinced her to stay on for another week. I must say young Louise is a fine woman.'

Josh's cheeks burned. 'I love the way y'all assume a grown man and woman can't manage their own romancing.'

'Don't be ungrateful,' Rose Ann chided.

'Joshua. Mrs Robertson Senior. Over here please.' Kathy beckoned for them to join her and for once Josh was relieved to be on the event coordinator's radar.

★　★　★

Louise came to the irrefutable conclusion that a lusciously tuxedoed Josh would make the perfect James Bond. She wouldn't deny that Chad looked

225

handsome too but something about Josh's implacable masculinity made her knees weaken.

'Why don't you find our table and fetch me a glass of champagne,' Audrey suggested. 'Then I'll set you free to drool over the caveman you're inexplicably in love with. I don't mind admitting Joshua is a good man. Solid and dependable. He can't help being big and — '

'Handsome. Rugged. Utterly male.'

Audrey's mouth turned up at the edges at Louise's description. 'Rose Ann hit the nail on the head when she first set eyes on you both.'

'Really.'

'Yes, really.' Audrey declared. 'What are all the people looking at over there?' She gestured toward a group of guests at the far end of the room.

Later she'd tell Josh that he'd been wrong. This room *did* impress her. The dark wood flooring, pale yellow walls, ornate white mouldings and ceiling were all perfectly set off by massive glittering chandeliers. Rich oil paintings graced the walls and stunning floral arrangements in subtle shades of cream and rose pink spaced around the room added to the beauty of the occasion. Filled with guests the room shimmered with life as it must have done when the Cheek family were in residence.

'It's an amazing video Josh put together with images from Cornwall and Tennessee all set to music he wrote himself.'

'In that case you had better help me over to see it.'

Louise hoped she'd have Audrey's determination and vibrant interest in life as she grew older.

'That dress suits you by the way. Your young man chose well.'

'Thank you.' She blushed. 'I wasn't sure.'

'Men know. At least all the best ones do. My dear husband enjoyed shopping with me and it's not the same without him.' Audrey's voice wobbled. 'You're a good girl. I admire anyone who works hard to overcome a difficult start in life.' The unexpected accolade took Louise by surprise. 'Don't argue. You know I don't give out undeserved praise.'

I'm gonna hug you too whether you like it or not. T. Ray's words flooded back. The surge of pleasure in Audrey's eyes when Louise gave her a brief hug satisfied her. They could all do with being more honest and she'd start with Josh. She refused to waste any more time.

21

He hadn't intended making the bride and groom cry.

'Oh, Josh, it's beautiful.' Maggie flung her arms around his neck and planted a wet kiss on his cheek. 'This is the best present ever you sneaky thing. Everyone loves it.'

Chad wiped at his eyes and clasped Josh's shoulder. 'If you tell me again that you can't help other veterans to express themselves through music I'll slap you around the head big time.'

'Am I out of the loop here?' Big J appeared with their mother.

'We'll talk later, Dad, and you too, Mom,' Josh promised. 'It's too complicated to go into now.' He was saved by the event organiser ringing a bell and asking everyone to take their seats for dinner. When no one was looking he'd shifted the place cards and slipped into the empty chair between Louise and Audrey. 'Is this the reject table, ladies? I've heard it's *the* place to be.' After the way Maggie and Chad met this was the new family joke.

'We don't consider ourselves rejected, do we Audrey? We're simply choosy with whom we sit.' Louise ladled on her most cutting British accent.

'You gonna choose me?' Josh whispered close to her ear.

'Maybe. If you're very lucky.'

'I'm already lucky. I'm sat here aren't I?'

Her amused gaze swept over him. 'It's funny but when I checked your mother's table plan earlier I could've sworn your cousin Pete's name was listed in that seat.'

'Your eye sight needs testing.'

'Very doubtful.'

'Are you complaining?' He teased a strand of silky hair back behind her ear. 'I thought not.'

'Stop being so smug.' The feeble protest amused Josh and he brushed a soft kiss over her warm cheek. 'You'd better let go of me because the food is coming.'

'Fair enough,' he conceded, 'at least for now.'

Louise picked up a plate. 'Anyone for a sausage roll?'

'What is it?' He peered at the small golden brown object. 'Chad warned me to avoid something but I can't remember what it was called.'

'Don't worry. For some reason he hates Scotch eggs but there aren't any today. Your brother made very few demands where the menu was concerned but that was non-negotiable.' She smiled. 'These are on Chad's approved list. They're sausage meat wrapped in puff pastry.'

'If you two could stop flirting for a minute I'd appreciate something to eat.' Audrey's pointed barb made them both laugh. After they'd tested the sausage rolls Louise reached for another long platter.

'Try a pasty.'

Josh wolfed down one miniature Cornish pasty and reached for another.

'These are good but you'll have to come to Cornwall and try the real thing,' Audrey said.

'I sure will if I'm invited?'

Louise muttered something under her breath.

'I didn't quite catch what you said.'

'Audrey just did.'

'Did what?'

'Invite you,' she hissed.

'And you?'

'Yes, and me. I'm inviting you too. Satisfied now?'

Josh squeezed her hand under the table. 'Very.'

'Oh look, they're bringing in the cake. Chad's going to be surprised. It's nearly time for your speech.'

The lead weight settling in the pit of his stomach had nothing to do with Emily's delicious pastry.

★ ★ ★

'Aren't Maggie and Chad so beautiful together?' Louise sighed. 'And that cake is divine.' The showstopper recreation of the ill-fated wedding cake — four tiers of almond sponge, fluffy white icing and fresh raspberries — was a triumph. 'Are you okay?' Josh's grim silence bothered her.

'I will be when this is over.' His hand tightened around a crumpled piece of paper.

'You'll be perfect. We've practised enough times and don't forget what I told you.'

'Imagine everyone naked,' he grunted. 'That's not gonna help.' Josh's hot gaze settled on her. 'At least not in your case.'

Checking that Audrey wasn't paying them any attention Louise nuzzled his neck. 'When this is over we'll have plenty of time alone.'

'For someone trying to calm me down you're doin' a lousy job.' Josh gave a wry smile. 'Kathy's giving me the evil eye.' He sighed and pushed back his chair. 'Wish me luck.'

Ignoring the fact nearly two hundred

people could be watching she cradled his face in her hands and indulged in a very thorough kiss. 'Off you go.'

'Yes, ma'am. How can I fail after that?'

She clutched her hands together as he made his way up to the front of the room and when Josh started to speak Louise silently recited the words along with him. She paused for laughs when he did and momentarily stopped breathing when he hesitated over a poignant childhood story. When he finished and asked everyone to rise and drink a toast to the bride and groom Louise was certain her legs would fail her.

'For goodness sake have a drink,' Audrey ordered. 'Joshua did an excellent job thanks to you.'

Louise beamed and drained her champagne in one swallow.

With the dinner over with she settled Audrey on a comfortable sofa with Rose Ann and waited until the first notes of 'Lady in Red' echoed through the room.

'They're playing our song.'

Swept into Josh's arms Louise became acutely aware of the press of his hard, warm body and softened into him.

'I can't be polite much longer. Not with you wearing red lace, smelling so wonderful and gazing at me that way.'

'What way would that be?' Louise stared into his eyes, shot through with golden fire and blazing into hers.

Josh stepped away and grabbed her hands. 'We're going to circulate and talk to people. Nobody will be able to complain I didn't do my best man duties properly but as soon as Maggie and Chad leave . . . all bets are off.'

'Good. Are you ready?'

'I've been ready since the moment we met, sweetheart.' Josh caressed her cheek with his calloused fingers.

There was nothing else to say.

★   ★   ★

Josh fingered the bunch of keys in his pocket. Chad slipped them into his hand earlier when they hung around the bar and waited for Maggie to get changed out of her wedding dress.

These are for my condo down in the Gulch. Help yourself. Just don't frighten the neighbours.

Would Louise feel pressured if he told her about Chad's offer? But if she discovered some other way she might come to the conclusion that he didn't want to . . .

'Are you free to give me a ride back to the house?'

He startled and stared at Louise. 'Yeah, of course. Everything's done. I've stowed the video equipment in my truck. Let's go.' They walked along in silence and reached the car park behind the museum.

'Is something wrong? You must be exhausted.'

Josh's pulse raced. 'I'm definitely not tired.' He shoved a hand up through his hair, exasperated at himself. 'Oh, shit, I'm lousy at this. I couldn't seduce a woman if I tried.'

Louise's tempting smile eased the

knot tying up his insides. 'If this is what not trying looks like keep doing it.' She slipped her arms around his waist and tugged him to her. 'It's working.'

'It is?' he croaked.

'Tell me what's on your mind.' Her cool, lush, voice trickled over him, seeping into every pore.

Josh pulled the keys from his pocket. 'Chad gave me these. They're to his condo. He thought I might want to get away from the house and . . . that we, um — '

'You have the best brother ever.' She smiled and gestured towards the truck. 'What are you waiting for?'

'Um, you to say yes or no? I don't want you to — '

'Stop talking and let's go.' Louise touched her finger to his lips. 'And yes I'm sure. Don't ask again or I might change my mind.'

He caught a flutter of anxiety in her voice but told himself everything would be fine.

22

Sizing up people and situations was second nature to Josh. The closer they came to the Gulch Louise's skin turned even paler and she clutched her slim white hands together on her lap. Logically he knew she wasn't frightened of him but the sight of her unease tore him up.

Josh kept the conversation light and told her all about the revived industrial area between Music Row and downtown. 'It's become the place to live for young professionals wanting an urban lifestyle. It wouldn't suit me. I like plenty of space.'

'I can't imagine Maggie settling here. Not after living in Cornwall.'

'From what Chad told me they'll only stay around long enough to find a house out in the country. They're going to hang on to Maggie's family home in

Cornwall as well and I'm guessing they'll cross the pond regularly.' He pointed out more of the restored buildings as they drove by. 'Those were all warehouses connected to the railroad but it stopped running back in the 1950s.' Josh pulled into Chad's assigned parking space next to the 12 South Flats building. 'Okay?'

'Of course.'

'His apartment is on the second floor.'

Louise chattered non-stop as they went in and while he gave her a quick tour of the condo. 'It's beautiful. Very modern.'

'But?'

'I prefer something more . . . comfortable. This reminds me of the pictures in glossy magazines. The ones that always look as though no one actually lives there.'

'Yeah, I get what you mean.'

She settled herself on the black leather sofa and wrapped her hands around her knees in a protective, childlike way. 'You're not stupid. You know I'm . . . ' Her breath hitched and Josh sat down next to her.

'Never be scared of me.'

Louise's pretty eyes glazed over and the pulse in her neck throbbed wildly. 'I'm not, Josh. I'm panicking because I'm no good at this.'

'This?'

'Sex. Making love. Whatever you want to call it.' She struggled to sound casual but he wasn't fooled. 'Craig told me I didn't have any clue how to please a man.'

'Did he make much of an effort to make it good for you?'

Louise shrugged. 'Not really. At least I don't think so.' Her colour deepened. 'I wasn't experienced enough to be sure.'

'When it's good it works both ways, honey.'

'I'd hate for you to be disappointed in me.'

He cradled her hands. 'I could never be disappointed in you. Ever.' Josh tried a different tack. 'You want to hear about every man's innate fear? We freak out that we won't match up to whatever mythical lover a woman's created in her imagination.'

'I would never do that to you. Kiss me.'

Louise's breathy plea aroused him all over again but he forced himself to slow down. One by one he pulled out the clips holding her hair in place. He ran his fingers through the fair silky strands and fanned them out over her shoulders.

'Your turn.' Josh steeled himself as she surrounded his mouth, teasing with her tongue until he let her in. When they came up for air Louise rested her hands on his chest.

'Do you mind if I undo your shirt?'

'Feel free.' Josh lay back on the sofa and sucked in his stomach as her trembling fingers worked at his buttons. 'Do you want me to take it off?' Louise nodded and he made fast work of getting rid of his shirt and tossing it to the floor. He slowly counted up to ten and back again as she placed her hand flat on his chest and explored his dark hair, running her fingers over the faded scars marring his skin.

'Will you tell me about them one day?'

He nodded. 'Whenever you want.' Josh hoped she got the idea that permission covered anything and everything.

'Should we go into the bedroom now?'

'There's no *should*. We can stay this way as long as you want or go back to Magnolia House. It's your choice. Always.'

★ ★ ★

A smile found its way out and she started to relax. 'I really wanted to tell you something at the reception but there was never a right moment.' Louise blushed. 'You truly *are* the best man ever and I think I do love you.' When he didn't speak she started to panic.

'Hey, don't fret.' Josh touched her

mouth. 'Smile at me that special way again and keep doing it. I'm stunned that's all. I never expected — '

'Me neither.'

A smile crept over his face. 'Back to your question.'

'Which one?' As he slid a finger under her shoulder strap Louise's skin heated with his touch.

'The one about the bedroom.'

'Oh, *that* one. I'm going with *should* on that one.'

'Thank God.' Josh's obvious relief made her laugh. 'I meant every word I said about it being your choice but I'm not gonna lie and pretend not to care either way.'

'Good. I promised I'd never be with another man who didn't love me and totally want to be with me.'

'I'm in on both counts.'

'I do believe it's time you took me to bed.'

'I'll be happy to oblige, Ms Louise.'

They walked hand in hand down the narrow hallway and inside the bedroom door Josh stopped. His tawny eyes gleamed as he rested his large hands on the curve of her shoulders. With slow deliberation he moved his hands down over her, tracing the contours of her body.

'Ever since we bought this dress I've imagined getting you out of it.' He eased Louise around with her back to him and scooped a handful of hair out of the way before pressing a soft kiss on her neck. 'Just so you know my imagination is pretty damn good.' The sound of the zipper inching down her back made Louise shudder and Josh slipped one hand inside to caress her bare skin. Pushing the dress down off her shoulders he allowed it to slip to the floor. 'Step out.'

She bent to take off her shoes.

'Leave them on. Please.'

'Oh. Okay if you want.' Louise couldn't refuse him anything.

'Well I'll be.' He swung her around to face him. 'My imagination's not as accurate as I thought. You're far more beautiful. I sure appreciate you carrying on the lace theme.' His shaking fingers rested on the delicate red bra Maggie had insisted she bought.

'Aren't you overdressed?' Louise suggested tentatively.

'No problem. I can soon remedy that.'

An instant searing blush heated her skin as he obeyed her request faster than she'd have thought possible. Solid, heavily muscled and marked by the signs of a hard outdoor life this wasn't a young man's body but only made her more attracted to him.

'I must remember never to give a military man orders unless I'm ready to face the consequences.'

'And are you ready?' He quirked one dark eyebrow and held out his hand. With a small nod Louise went to him.

★   ★   ★

'Wow. If that was you being lousy keep it up. You've about finished me off in the best possible way.' Josh chuckled. 'I'd say we well and truly laid the ghost of that idiot to rest.' Louise went stiff in his arms. 'I say it like it is. You know that.'

'I do, and I'm thankful, really.'

'Prove it.'

'How?'

'Let me love you again.'

'I'm game if you are.'

Josh didn't need asking twice.

'I do believe I'm getting the hang of this.' Louise mumbled into his chest a little while later. He hoped he wasn't crushing her because he couldn't see himself moving anytime soon.

'Yeah, I'd say you are.' He turned his head and glanced at the bedside clock — a fancy stainless steel design with dots instead of regular numbers. 'Trust my idiot brother not to have a clock you can read.'

'Oh my God, it's five o'clock in the morning,' Louise shrieked. 'We fell asleep. They'll all be awake soon and we'll wander in wearing yesterday's clothes and everyone will know what — '

Josh stopped her with a kiss.

'Breathe. Calm down. I told Jonathan where we were going in case anyone needed us. I didn't want them to panic and send out a search party.'

'That's thoughtful of you. At least I think it is.'

'We're both well over the age of consent. It's our private business and no one else's. There are a few people — namely Audrey and my grandmother — who might disagree but we'll deal with them.'

'You know what? I think we can deal with anything.' Louise smiled and pushed him down on his back. 'As we say in England — in for a penny in for a pound.'

'Is that the same as 'might as well be hung for a sheep as a lamb'?'

'Probably.'

'We still need to sample Chad's shower. He keeps bragging how many jets it has and I've got a fancy to check it out.'

'You're a very wicked man.'

'Only with you, sweetheart, only with you.' Josh shut his mouth before he could spoil the moment. If he dared mention the future and how they'd work out the details of long-distance loving they'd be forced to face up to reality and he wasn't sure they were ready.

23

Josh leaned against the kitchen counter and waited for the coffee machine, desperate for caffeine.

'I've been looking for you.' Audrey limped in, leaning heavily on her ornate ebony walking stick. He guessed she'd overdone it at yesterday's wedding but he wasn't stupid enough to ask. Josh suspected he was on target to receive a lecture about not breaking Louise's heart. 'You'll be very surprised to hear who telephoned me last evening.'

'Make my day.'

The hint of a smile tugged at her mouth. 'Our least favourite art dealer.'

'Merton?'

'From what I gather he does a lot of business in America these days and happens to be in Nashville at the moment. He met a mutual acquaintance of ours at the Frist Center and

Frederick Lyle happened to mention I was here on a visit.'

'But why would he call you?' It didn't make any sense to Josh. 'You're hardly best buddies.'

'Because his greed won out over common sense.' Audrey smirked. 'He's idiotic enough to assume I'll ignore our past disagreements and be interested in purchasing a particular item he's got for sale.'

'Moron.'

'Not completely.' She shook her head. 'I'm ashamed to admit when he claimed to have in his possession an original Josef Lorenzl Art Deco ballerina sculpture I had a momentary wobble before giving myself a stiff talking to.'

Josh suppressed a smile. Audrey wasn't only hard on other people. 'You said he 'claimed to be'?'

'They're extremely rare. In all my years of being an Art Deco aficionado I've only seen one outside of a museum and that belonged to an obscenely wealthy Saudi prince.'

'What did you tell Merton?'

'I invited him to pay a visit to me tomorrow. The house should be quiet enough for our purposes. Maggie and Chad are on their way to the Caribbean and Emily and her little family will be flying to New York after lunch today. I understand they're doing some sightseeing before they cross the Atlantic again next week.' She held up a warning finger. 'Do not even begin to get any ideas involving doing Mr Merton physical harm. We're much smarter than that.'

'Are we?'

'Of course.' Audrey sat down with obvious relief and winced as she rubbed her left knee. 'He's unaware that Louise works for me now and won't discover that pertinent fact until the right moment.'

Josh poured his coffee and joined her. 'What's your plan?'

'I suppose I should have asked first but I shared the necessary information with your father. He's been most useful checking out things on the internet for me.'

'Does Louise know?'

'Does Louise know what?' His favourite lady breezed into the kitchen and leaned in to give him a kiss on the cheek. 'What are you up to? Something nice I hope.'

Josh caught Audrey's eye and she gave a shrug. This was up to him. 'Sit down, sweetheart.'

'What's wrong?'

'Nothing serious.' He held her hands. 'I need you to listen to me.' He'd promised to be truthful and refused to fall at the first hurdle. Josh calmly repeated Audrey's story and tightened his grasp when she tried to jerk away. 'We were discussing what to do and need your opinion.'

'I should've been told first. How many other people know?'

'Sweetheart, don't be too — '

'She's quite right, Joshua.' Audrey sunk into a heavy sigh. 'My dear husband always said my worse fault was my implacable belief that I knew better than other people how they should run their lives.' Her tired, grey face showed every one of her seventy-five years this morning. 'Of course he loved me anyway but — '

'So do we.' Josh's blunt statement made both women stare. 'Deep down Louise knows you wouldn't have interfered if you didn't love her too. Aren't I right?' He mentally crossed his fingers. For several long seconds her stony glare remained fixed in place.

'I suppose so,' she conceded. 'I'm sorry, Audrey.'

'I deserved it.'

'No, you didn't. You've been wonderfully kind to me and I shouldn't have spoken to you that way.'

'It's forgotten.' Audrey's brisk manner made it clear she'd heard enough sentimental talk for one day. 'Remember the old saying about revenge being a dish best served cold. Our Mr Merton believes he's got away with his appalling behaviour but it's time to prove him wrong. Will you listen to our ideas, my dear?'

'I suppose so.'

'I promise none involve any form of physical violence against Mr. Merton.'

'Pity.' Josh interjected.

'That is definitely *not* an option.' Louise declared with the hint of a smile.

'Joshua's father discovered that the small sculpture Merton is trying to sell me for a quarter of a million pounds is almost certainly a fake.' Audrey explained. 'He reluctantly agreed to bring another expert here tomorrow afternoon and I'll give Mr Merton no choice but to allow Miss Wolfe to check out the piece before I consider whether or not to buy.'

Louise frowned. 'I can see this blowing apart his reputation in the art community but it won't stop him preying on other gullible women.'

'Don't you dare to call yourself that,' Josh protested. 'We all make mistakes. I've made enough to fill a whole set of encyclopaedias.'

Audrey pulled out a sheaf of papers from her handbag. 'Thanks to a very discreet private detective I managed to contact three of Mr Merton's previous assistants and these letters detail his unwelcome approaches to each of them.'

'I'm not going to court. I can't.' Louise's eyes widened.

'Don't worry. The other young ladies only agreed to confide in my contact on the condition that we didn't involve the police.' She leaned back in the chair and gave a sly smile. 'But Mr Merton doesn't need to know that, does he?'

'You devious . . . ' Josh barely managed to stop himself from calling her something he shouldn't.

Audrey frowned. 'Louise, you'll have to be tough and face him again.'

'But not on your own. I'll be with you,' Josh hurried to reassure her.

'We don't need — '

'She does this with me there or not at all.' Josh worried he'd gone too far but Louise cracked a faint smile.

'We'll do it.'

'I suppose that will still work,' Audrey conceded and slotted the papers back in her handbag. 'I'd like your help now for a while, Louise, and then you're free for the rest of the day. Tricia is taking Rose Ann and me for a drive out to a local vineyard. We'll have lunch there and sample some of the wines.'

'Of course.'

After the two women left Josh poured himself another mug of coffee. He'd got some serious thinking to do before the meeting with Merton.

⋆　⋆　⋆

Her scissors hovered above the pair of jeans spread out on her bed. She'd never consider doing such a crazy thing unless everybody else was safely out of the house. Louise sucked in a deep breath and cut through the soft well-worn denim. Josh had smiled quietly when she asked where they were going and only said that she needed to be casually dressed. Five minutes later she tidied up the shorn-off hems and tugged on the incredibly short shorts. Louise examined herself objectively in the mirror. *Really?*

Josh let out a long low whistle as she walked down the stairs. 'Boy, you sure do those Daisy Dukes proud.'

'I'm glad I didn't sacrifice a decent pair of jeans in vain.'

'You sure didn't. Trust me you'll be repaid in heaven.' He made a grab for her and yanked Louise up against him. 'Or sooner if you're a real good girl.'

'Sooner works for me.' She laughed and kissed his cheek. 'Where are we going? Are you going to let me in on the secret now?'

'Apart from the nearest bed?' His cheeky question earned him a poke in the ribs. 'I'm taking you out to Leiper's Fork and showing you the land I've got plans for.' He shifted his hands to circle her hips. 'I've got plans for you too.'

'You would. Let's go.' Louise slipped from his arms and walked towards the door with a swing to her step.

'It's a pretty day. You'll enjoy the drive.'

'I love you so it's all good.'

'It sure is.' Josh's smile melted her all over again. 'Hop in.'

Once they escaped the Nashville traffic the half-hour drive took in some of the loveliest countryside she'd seen on the whole trip. Lush farmland, miles of neat white fences, traditional houses with wraparound porches, red-painted barns and the ever-present American flags flying in the breeze.

'Here we are. This is the original Robertson land.' They bumped their way down a rough gravel track and he pulled the truck to a stop in front of a dilapidated log cabin. 'This is all that's left of the original house.' He rested his hands on the steering wheel. 'I wrote a lot of songs out here as a teenager. I'd sneak off after another fight with my dad and when things fell apart with Ellen I retreated here to think.'

'You haven't been back for a while?'

'No.' Josh shook his head. 'I guess I associated it with rough times.'

'I think it will be perfect for other people's rough times.'

He slid his hands up through her loose hair and pulled her close enough to kiss. 'You are so goddamn beautiful.'

'You are too.'

'Men on the covers of glossy magazines are beautiful. I've been around the block far too many times and lived too hard a life to qualify.'

'But you're beautiful to me in the same way I am to you.' Louise insisted. 'Other men might not notice me and another woman might pass you by without a second glance.' Her hand centred on his chest and pressed against his soft T-shirt. 'In here you're the most beautiful man in the world.'

Josh stroked his fingers over her cheek. 'You floor me every time. My dumb seventeen-year-old self thought I understood all about love but it took me another twenty-three years to discover the real thing.'

'How about we go inside and you show me the house?' Louise suggested. Sharing their emotions was difficult for them both. 'Talk me through your plans.' The wicked glint in his eyes made her laugh and she smacked his arm. 'For the music therapy centre. I know about your other ones.'

'You really don't, honey, but you will soon.' His enigmatic response flustered her and Josh hooked his arm through hers. 'By the way they're dreams. Plan is too practical a word.' He stopped at the bottom of the rickety steps. 'I want to salvage everything we can when we rebuild because this is where it all began.' Josh face darkened. 'Healing takes time and music helps because it doesn't judge. It crosses all boundaries.'

Silent gratitude to Chad swept through her for bringing his brother back to where he clearly belonged. 'Lead the way.'

'With you along for the ride I'm pretty sure I can do anything.' Josh's simple heartfelt words brought tears to her eyes. In companionable silence they picked their way up the broken steps and began to map out Josh's dream.

24

Louise's nerves hummed and she re-checked her watch.

'He'll be late. His sort always are,' Josh drawled. 'Remember we're not going in until my dad comes through to fetch us.'

They'd gone over the plan multiple times but even after five long years she still couldn't visualise facing Craig again. She jumped at the dull thud of the front door knocker and Josh rested his hand on her shoulder. Louise listened to the voices and picked out Craig's smooth English accent and Big J's hearty southern one.

'I'm sure Audrey's ready to give an Oscar-worthy performance.' Josh grinned. 'Merton's going to regret coming when we're through with him.' He drew Louise to him for a long satisfying kiss. 'You'll be able to put this behind you and move on. It's the only way.'

'Like you and T. Ray?'

'Yep.' A shadow flitted across his face. 'I convinced myself I'd done the wrong thing in saving him and the relief is mind-blowing.'

The voices in the hall went quiet.

'Do you want a cup of tea? I've been taking instruction,' Josh offered.

'Thanks but I couldn't swallow a thing. I'm sorry.'

'I'm the one who's sorry. This isn't my forte. I'm better with action.'

Louise couldn't help laughing. 'So I'd noticed.'

'See I made you smile again. If all else fails remind a woman you're hot in bed.'

'Did it work with all the others too?'

'None of . . . ' Josh wagged his finger. 'Oh, boy, you're good. You reel me in every time.' The door flew open and his father stepped into the room.

'Merton's wriggling like a worm on a hook and Miss Wolfe's got him by the balls.' Big J's face turned scarlet. 'I sure am sorry, Louise, forgot my manners.'

'Please don't apologise. I kicked him there the last time we met.'

'Good woman. If you want it doing again let us know.' He gestured to Josh. 'I'm sure this one would be happy to oblige.' Big J headed for the door. 'Let's go and wait in the hall until Audrey rings the bell.'

Louise's feet remained glued to the floor.

'We'll do this together.' Josh repeated her words back at her, the same ones she'd encouraged him with at the Bluebird Cafe.

'Yes, we will.' She took a deep breath and walked out between the two men with her head held high.

Craig's incredulous voice drifted out through the half-open door. 'You must be insane. Sexual harassment. Attempted rape? Where on earth did you get such ridiculous ideas from?'

'She got them from me.' Louise burst into the room followed by Josh and his father, too angry to wait any longer.

'Louise? What in heaven's name are

you doing here?'

'Oh, did I forget to mention Miss Giles has been working for me ever since she left your . . . employment?' Audrey's razor-sharp tone made Louise swallow a bubble of laughter.

'I suppose this charade is your way of getting revenge because I ended our personal relationship?' He sneered. 'We both know your general incompetence at the job forced me to let you go.'

The scathing retort would've shaken the old Louise but she plastered on a condescending smile and prepared to shred Craig Merton into tiny pieces.

★ ★ ★

Josh wouldn't care to be in the other man's shoes. God, he loved the strength of this woman. No one apart from him would guess she was shaking inside.

'I'm afraid we remember things differently.' Her quasi-sweet tone would've given her away to anyone who understood her but Merton continued to smirk.

You idiot. 'I accept I was naive to fall for your lame seduction techniques but when you made it clear I didn't meet your . . . standards around the same time as I started to question the ethics of your business transactions I got suspicious.' Louise stood in front of the Englishman. 'When I discovered several of your previous assistants all left abruptly I found out there were plenty of rumours flying around that you expected a lot more than computer skills from your female employees.'

'We've already discussed the un-savoury stories I dug up, haven't we, Mr Merton?' Audrey interrupted. 'Your reputation in the European art commu-nity is already shaky and Mr Robertson Senior confirmed for me that the same concerns have begun to spread here to America.' She picked up a small bronze ballerina from the table. 'Miss Wolfe gave us her expert opinion on this piece before she left and quite frankly called you a cheat. Do you have anything to say for yourself?'

Merton blustered and attempted to insist that he'd made a genuine mistake about the sculpture.

'I'm sure none of us believe that for one moment. As a matter of interest what about Fiona James, Jocelyn Ward and Mary Browning? Were they all incompetent research assistants too?' Louise pressed.

Audrey thrust a handful of papers at Merton. 'These would suggest that *you* are the unsatisfactory one.'

He barely glanced at the emails before tossing them on the table. 'These prove nothing. No court would find me guilty.'

'You sure about that, pal?' Josh interrupted.

'And who on earth might you be?'

'I'm Big J's oldest son. Josh Robertson. Major Joshua Claiborne Robertson, retired US Army if we're splitting hairs.' His drawl deepened.

Merton's glacial stare shifted to Louise. 'Ah now I see the way the wind is blowing. For an uneducated brat you've made quite a catch.'

Josh stiffened.

'Don't give him the satisfaction. He's a dick,' his father whispered, guessing that his oldest son was close to slamming his fist into Craig Merton's face.

Two red angry spots lit up Louise's cheeks. 'Absolutely. Josh has integrity, honesty, intelligence and a great sense of humour.' She reckoned them up on her fingers. 'What woman wouldn't prefer those traits to devious, self-satisfied and scheming?' A wicked smile pulled at her mouth. 'Mr Robertson and Audrey you might want to cover your ears.' She pinned Merton with her blazing eyes. 'He's also excellent in bed. I had no idea what I was missing. You should take some lessons.'

Josh couldn't decide whether to kiss her senseless or crawl under the nearest chair.

'You vicious little tramp.'

He'd never heard such a satisfying sound as Louise's hand connecting with Merton's cheek in a stinging slap.

'Bravo.' Josh's long, slow hand clap earned him another disparaging glare from Merton.

'What are you after? Money?' Merton rubbed at the red mark blooming on his face and glanced scathingly around the room. 'I can't imagine why. It's hardly in short supply around here.'

That question proved how little this man understood Louise. She was the furthest thing from a gold digger he'd ever met and if anything the Robertson family money freaked her out.

'All I want is justice.' Her quiet statement tore at Josh's heart. 'For myself and the other women you've wronged and all the people you've tricked with your underhand sales techniques.'

'If I leave the antiques business and take early retirement in the south of France will that satisfy you?'

To Josh that didn't sound much of a hardship but he held his tongue.

'Yes, as long as you also repay all the money you've taken under false pretences.' Louise replied. 'To save myself and the women from testifying in court they're willing to accept a written apology from you and a measure of financial compensation. We also expect you to make a full written confession to be kept by us in a safe place and used if it becomes necessary.'

'But how will I know — '

'You won't.'

'I suppose you leave me with no choice,' Merton conceded with a grimace.

Audrey turned to Josh's father. 'I believe we can deal with the details and let these two young people go.'

'We sure can, ma'am,' Big J agreed.

'Are you happy with that?' Josh asked Louise, not wanting to assume anything.

She gave Merton a cool appraising stare. 'Your greed pulled you down in the end. I knew it would if I was patient.' Her tear-filled eyes rested on Josh. 'Take me out of here, please, I need some fresh air.'

'No problem.' He whisked her back

into the hall and didn't speak until they were outside in the garden and he'd kissed her thoroughly. 'Is that better?'

'You always know what I need.'

'But?'

'Why do you think there's one of those?'

'Because I can hear it.' He took a stab. 'It's the money, isn't it?' Louise shrugged. 'Perhaps you could donate your portion of Merton's compensation to a charity for abused women?'

'That's a great idea.'

He might as well get something else out in the open while they were talking about money. 'The Robertson fortune is a different story.'

'I know.' Louise sighed. 'It honestly didn't click until Audrey pointed it out. I must be dumb. I never — '

'I know you didn't and love you all the more for it. I can't get around the fact that I'll inherit half of all this one day. Although I don't want to work in Robertson Guitars I'll still share responsibility for it along with Chad. There's no point in sugar coatin' it.'

'In other words — love you and what comes along with you?'

'Yep. We've both got baggage, sweetheart. That's life.' Josh gave her a gentle kiss. 'Can you handle it?'

'If you can handle an uneducated brat who's also a vicious little tramp.'

'Merton sure has a way with words.' Josh laughed. 'Remind me never to cross you. That slap you gave him was a real doozy.'

'A what?'

'Something unexpected. Don't you have doozies in England?'

Louise grinned. 'We'd probably say it came out of the blue.'

'That works.' Josh suddenly remembered where the conversation started. 'So are you in?'

'In what?'

'The whole baggage thing?' She frowned, obviously unsure what exactly he was asking. 'I guess I'm sayin' are you happy to carry on exploring this love thing and see where it leads us?'

'Sounds wonderful to me.'

'I need you by my side when I talk to my folks tonight.' Josh struggled to keep his emotions under control. 'I need their support.' He rested two fingers on her lips before she could speak. 'I know I mentioned plans and got all vague on you but some are gonna be hazy for a while. Are you okay with that?'

'Don't you think the term 'work in progress' sounds more grown-up?'

'Whatever you say is fine by me.' He grinned. 'Did I get that part right? Chad drummed it into me.'

'You're a fast learner.'

'Good. This 'work-in-progress' suggests we go back to the house and move forward with the next part of the plan.'

'And this one totally agrees.'

Josh hoped she'd agree with him on a whole lot more before long.

25

Josh couldn't blame his parents for appearing stunned after he declared his intention to turn their old, abandoned family land into a music therapy centre. It must be something they'd never have considered him doing in a million years. 'Chad came up with idea. He was really impressed when he visited the one here in Nashville and thought it would be a good match for me. I'm sure once you see the work they're doing it'll all make more sense.' He kept going. 'I reckon you'll say this is way out in left field but I'm in love with this beautiful lady and when the time's right I hope she'll marry me.' Louise's jaw dropped but before she could say anything his father burst out laughing.

'I'm startin' to get why your mother thinks we're alike. You go all out when you want something and I'm the same way.' He seized his wife's hand. 'I saw this pretty little gal at a party when we were sixteen. I pushed out of the way the loser she was dancing with and told her she was my partner now.'

'He was brash. Cocky. And drop-dead handsome.' Tricia's indulgent reply made his father blush. 'That evening he told your granddaddy he planned to marry me on my eighteenth birthday.'

'I did too, didn't I?'

'You broke up Ellen and me because you saw we didn't have what you and Mom share,' Josh mused. 'Why didn't you just say so?'

'Because he's useless at expressing his emotions,' Tricia chipped in.

'Wow that sounds like someone else I know,' Louise observed with a teasing smile. 'I've actually discovered thumb-screws work quite well for extracting information.'

'Do you get the feeling we're being ganged up on?' Josh's teasing observation brought a smile to his father's face.

'That's why we need to stick together

instead of butting heads all the time.' Big J was as blunt as ever. 'I don't expect you to take over the business but Chad's gonna need support one day and *I* must know you'll give it to him.'

'I will,' Josh promised. 'You've always been there for me even when I told you where you could stick your help. I owe you big time.' He tightened his grip on Louise's hand. 'I've got to go back to Colorado and sort things out there but I'll be back as soon as I can.'

'Hug him you know you want to.' Tricia poked his father's arm.

'Hey I'll do it if he won't.' Josh strode across and threw his arms around his father before letting go again with a tight smile. 'I reckon that'll do us for another decade or so, don't you?'

'Works for me.' Big J growled.

'What are your plans for the rest of the week?'

Josh wasn't sure how to answer his mother's question because everything was down to Louise and he couldn't ask her in front of everyone.

'It all depends on Audrey.' She stepped in to his rescue. 'I mustn't abuse her kindness and totally forget I'm working for her. Josh understands.'

'I can run y'all around anywhere you want,' Josh winked at his father, 'although I might need to borrow some decent transportation. I can't see me hauling Audrey in my beat-up truck.'

'Take the Cadillac. It's got enough room to fit in your mother and Rose Ann too 'cause I'm guessing you'll be saddled with them all.'

'Thanks.' His voice must have conveyed a mixture of trepidation and pleasure because everyone laughed.

'It's been a busy day. I'm ready for bed.' His mother glared at his father when Big J opened his mouth to object.

'Oh, yeah, I'm tired too. We'll see you kids in the morning.'

Josh hoped Louise wouldn't get the idea to join them. Not yet.

★ ★ ★

'Isn't going from a 'work-in-progress' to marriage a bit of a leap?' Louise's voice trembled.

'I did say when the time's right,' Josh protested. 'You sure do rattle my cage and make me say things without thinking them through. I get that I spoke out of turn but I wanted my folks and you to know how I feel.'

'Being mature adults shouldn't we be wary about rushing into things?'

'Don't know about you, sweetheart, but I'm not *quite* over the hill.' Josh shifted closer and wrapped his arms around her. 'We know our own minds.'

'But do we?' She persisted. 'I've had no experience in building a strong family life and the one man I dared to take a chance on turned out to be a womanising crook.' Louise bit back tears.

'I've made a load of mistakes too and you know I'm no saint. I think our first priority is an early trip to Cornwall. I want to see this place y'all rave about.'

'The sooner the better.' She took

several deep breaths. 'Would you mind coming with me to visit Jules? I need to at least try to put things right with her.'

'No problem.' A hint of uncertainty darkened his smile. 'I'm not sure how Audrey will take it but after I've been to Cornwall would you consider coming back here again? Maybe stay longer this time and think about our, um, options?'

'You're such a military man sometimes.' She couldn't help laughing. 'And there's nothing wrong with that.'

Josh flushed. 'Chad inherited Mom's smooth charm but I'm more like my dad because he sure doesn't have much either.'

'All I need is a man who says what he means and keeps his promises.' She smiled. 'If I want red roses I'll buy my own.'

'I'll grow roses for you, sweetheart. Gardening I can do. But nothing I grow will be as beautiful as you.'

'How can you say you're not a romantic when you come out with things like that?'

Josh looked puzzled. 'Because it's a fact. I didn't make it up to impress you.'

'It did anyway.'

'Whatever works.'

★ ★ ★

For every precious moment of their extra week together Josh had ordered himself to live in the moment. That still left him standing at the Nashville airport on a rainy Monday morning feeling like his world was ending. Louise nestled in his arms and her obvious sadness seeped into his heart.

'Don't try to be cheerful. I couldn't stand it.' Her muffled whisper tore at him and he breathed in her soft musky scent, imprinting it on his mind.

'No problem. I can do miserable.'

'Me too.'

He glanced over her shoulder. 'Audrey's waving her umbrella at you.'

'I should go.'

'Three weeks.'

'That's five hundred and four hours

279

or thirty thousand two hundred and forty minutes — right?' Louise's smoky grey eyes shimmered with the ghost of a smile. 'Not that I've worked it out or anything.'

'Nah, of course not. Me neither.' He sighed and seized her mouth in a deep kiss, full of heat and promise. 'I love you.'

'I love you too and I've decided I don't care if that's crazy or illogical.'

'I'm not good enough for you and never will be but — '

'Don't you dare say that again.' She raised her voice. Everyone around them stared. 'You're the best man ever. *My* best man. Do you get it now?'

'I believe we're all perfectly aware of it now, my dear. Announcing it to the whole world has that effect.' Audrey interrupted but not unkindly. 'I'm sorry but we have a plane to catch.' She fixed her piercing gaze on Josh. 'Don't worry. Louise is a fine woman and she'll sort you out.'

He loosened his hold on Louise and

planted a loud, smacking kiss on Audrey's cheek. 'She sure will and we'll always consider you our fairy godmother.'

'You're a very cheeky man and no better than your brother. I'll see you in Cornwall.'

'That's a date.' He turned back to Louise. 'Go now before I change my mind about letting you go.'

Louise squeezed his hand and kissed him one last time.

Five hundred and four hours and counting.

26

Josh kept his fingers crossed that Louise wouldn't complain if he turned up in Cornwall a week early. He refused to wait another one hundred and sixty-eight hours to see her again.

He'd asked his neighbour in Colorado to keep an eye on his land until Josh came to a long-term decision on the property. After his trip out west he'd loaded up his car and returned to Nashville where he spent an intense week learning everything he could about the music therapy programmes for veterans already in place. It'd helped him make a lot of contacts and he'd started to garner backing for his plans.

'Your mother tells me you're leaving after lunch.' Big J strolled into the kitchen and grabbed an apple from the bowl.

Another thing we've got in common.

'Didn't think you'd be able to wait.' His father laughed. 'I heard on the grapevine you've got a ring?'

'Yeah. You don't think I'm rushing Louise?' For a second his father gave him an unreadable stare. He'd never asked for advice before.

'Probably but that's never stopped any Robertson man. I'm pretty sure the lady won't mind.' His eyes narrowed. 'Don't you dare do anything dumb and run off with Louise to Gretna Green. Your mother will never forgive you.'

'Would you?' The idea of eloping sounded pretty tempting. 'That's a stupid question. You've forgiven a lot worse.'

Big J shrugged. 'True, but this would hurt your mother and grandmother big time.'

'I promise we won't do anything dumb but don't bank on a fancy wedding like Chad and Maggie's.'

'Louise might not agree.'

A cold trickle of panic inched down his spine.

'Get a grip, boy. You won't know until you ask. Maybe she'll turn you down.'

'Don't — '

'I'm joking. Louise is plainly nuts about you although God knows why and he sure ain't telling.' His father chuckled.

'You're damn right there.'

'When you've got your bag packed I'll run you to the airport. I'm gonna make sure you don't chicken out.'

'I'll get you back for that lousy joke one day.' He hurried away with his father's laughter ringing in his ears.

★ ★ ★

'I need you to meet the three o'clock train this afternoon at St. Erth. A ceramics collector friend of mine is coming down from London and will be staying with us for a few days.' Audrey glanced up from reading the newspaper and peered at Louise over her half-moon glasses.

'Today? Oh, of course. Who is it?'

'Marigold Dunstan. You haven't met her before but I'm sure the two of you will get on well.'

'I'll check the spare bedroom is tidy and freshen up the bathroom.' Audrey usually gave her advance warning of any guests but presumably she'd forgotten this time.

'That's a good idea.' Audrey returned to her newspaper but Louise noticed the tiny smile hanging around her mouth and wondered what put it there.

After clearing away lunch she set off with a shopping list, leaving early enough to make a stop at the supermarket on her way to the railway station. It'd been impossible to pin Audrey down about what Miss Dunstan might prefer to eat so she'd decided to take the easy way out and buy a ready-roasted chicken and cook a selection of fresh vegetables to go with it.

Louise made it to St. Erth station with five minutes to spare and snagged the last open space in the small car park. She walked across the pedestrian bridge to wait on the platform. Audrey's unhelpful description of her friend as middle-aged with short brown hair starting to turn grey made her hope there wouldn't be too many single travellers fitting the same vague criteria.

The train pulled in on time and she scanned up and down the platform as people started to get off.

'Lookin' for someone?'

Louise would've collapsed if Josh hadn't wrapped his strong arms around her and held her upright. 'What on earth — '

'Marigold Dunstan at your service, ma'am.' Josh grinned. She couldn't decide whether to hit him or kiss him but he took the decision out of her hands and it was several minutes before she could breathe properly again.

'You and Audrey plotted this between you, didn't you?'

A broad smile spread across his rugged, handsome face. 'Guilty as charged. She did her fairy godmother piece again and helped me out.'

'I thought you weren't coming until next week.'

'Couldn't wait any longer.'

Tears seeped out of her eyes and trickled down her cheeks.

'Oh, heck, don't cry.'

'They're happy tears, you idiot. It's been awful . . . but I couldn't abandon Audrey and rush back to Nashville.'

Josh cupped his hand behind her neck and drew her to him for another lingering kiss. 'That's why I came to you.' He glanced around. 'I suppose this is a decent enough place. It'll have to do.'

'What for?'

He kissed the tip of her nose. 'Stop asking so many questions. It sure is hard for a guy to pull off a surprise around you.'

'You've done a pretty good job so far.'

'I'm not finished yet.' He fumbled in his trouser pocket and dropped down to one knee.

'Is something wrong with your

leg . . . ' Louise's voice caught in her throat. She glanced around them and a hot furious blush raced up her neck to make her face burn. Everyone remaining on the platform stopped what they were doing and openly stared in their direction.

Josh flipped open a small white box and a stunning diamond ring glittered in the sunshine. 'You were in line to get a romantic proposal tomorrow but I can't wait. Sorry. You know I'm a simple man. I love you, Louise, and I want you to be my wife. Marry me.'

'I don't know what to say, I — '

The gold flecks in his eyes brightened. 'There're two choices, yes or no, it's not rocket science. Don't overthink this,' he pleaded.

She pushed away the myriad of questions she could ask because only one truly mattered. *Do you love this man and want to spend the rest of your life loving and being loved by him?* 'Of course I will,' she laughed, 'did you ever doubt I'd say yes?'

Loud claps and cheers erupted around them and her new fiancé playfully bowed to the small crowd.

'No, I wouldn't have raced four thousand miles otherwise.' Josh seized her hand. 'I hope you're okay with the ring. It stirred up a big discussion among my family. Maggie begged me not to choose it myself. Chad said I had to. My grandmother wanted to give me her own engagement ring to use. In the end my mom stepped in and ordered me to buy the biggest diamond I could afford and go for it. She figured it didn't matter if you usually preferred to keep things simple — apparently engagement rings are different and you'll want to show it off like any other woman.'

'Goodness, I'd no idea a Robertson family engagement was such a communal effort.' She checked out the ring as Josh eased it out of the box. 'Your mother is an extremely smart lady.' The large rectangular diamond set in a wide platinum band was stunning. 'Oh wow, it's definitely show-off able.' Josh slipped the ring on her finger and kissed it into place.

'Can I get up now? My forty-year-old knees are protesting.'

'Come on, old man.' Louise laughingly helped him up. 'I need to keep you in good shape for running around after our children.'

'We've never mentioned kids.' His raspy voice betrayed him. 'I wasn't sure if you'd want any, not after . . . well the tough time you had growing up.'

Josh's sweetness touched her. His rugged exterior masked the kindest heart of any man she'd ever met. 'Until you came along I wasn't sure but now I can't imagine anything better.' She melted into his arms, soaking up the warmth and strength she'd recognised the first day they met. 'I assume you — '

'Heck, yes. If we're lucky enough, and if not you'll be more than I need for a great life.'

'We'll have to wait and see like everyone else.' Louise swallowed hard. 'If we don't get back to Audrey soon she'll wonder what's happened to 'Marigold Dunstan.'' She prodded his arm. 'I cleaned the spare bedroom ready for 'her'.'

'Do you think Audrey's gonna object if I whisk you away to a hotel?' He tightened his hold on her waist. 'I sure didn't travel all this way to sleep alone.'

'I doubt she'll object to very much where you're concerned. Audrey turns into a different woman around you and your brother.'

'Must be our southern charm,' he quipped, thickening his soft drawl.

Oh, you have no idea. You're oblivious and I love you all the more for it.

'Come on. Let's stun our fairy god-mother with this dazzler.' His rich laughter and broad smile combined to make Louise even happier — something she wouldn't have thought possible.

Together they headed off into the sunshine.

27

Springtime in Cornwall — Nine months later

'I can't believe you asked for those gut-bombs,' Chad groused. He poked a finger at the plate of Scotch eggs on the buffet table.

Two Hearts Catering was back in business for one day only. Maggie and Emily had worked non-stop for the last week to produce a selection of Louise and Josh's Cornish and American favourites for today's wedding reception.

'They're good stuff so stop your bitchin'. We've got everything from Cornish pasties to good ole country ham biscuits and fried chicken so find something you *do* like.' Josh dismissed his brother's complaint and picked up one of the offending objects to pop into his mouth. 'I'm off to snatch back my bride.'

'Yeah, you've been apart all of five minutes.'

'Oh yeah and who keeps checking on his pregnant wife?'

Chad flushed. 'Maggie might not feel well or something.'

'You'll drive the woman crazy long before July.'

'When it's your turn you'll understand,' Chad retorted. When Josh didn't instantly respond he broke into a wide grin. 'Whoa. Did I put my foot in it?'

'Both of 'em,' Josh muttered. 'If you say a word to anyone you're a dead man. I swore to Louise we'd keep it a secret until we come back from honeymoon.'

'You old devil,' he chuckled, 'so much for Mr Cautious.'

Because they'd been certain it would take a while they'd been less than careful. Josh could still picture Louise's embarrassment when she told him on Valentine's Day that if all went well they'd be parents in September.

'My lips are sealed,' Chad promised. A glazed expression crossed his face.

'Our kids will grow up together. How cool is that? We won't let them drift apart like we stupidly did for a while there.'

Josh's throat tightened and he couldn't have spoken if he'd been offered a million dollars.

'There you are.' Louise appeared by his elbow and glanced between the pair of them. 'Are you two having a brother moment?'

'How's my new sister-in-law doing? Beautiful as ever I see.' Chad swiftly changed the subject. 'Are you glad we told you about this place?' He gestured around the room.

They'd insisted they wanted a small, intimate wedding but couldn't decide where until Maggie and Chad suggested Polvennor House, known forever as the site of the infamous reject table and cake disaster wedding reception. The small Victorian country house hotel instantly appealed to them and today the beautiful building was at its best, highlighted with stunning arrangements of early Cornish spring flowers including the first magnolias, hundreds of daffodils and vibrant blue rhododendrons.

'It's perfect,' Louise agreed. 'I'm so pleased your grandmother could come.'

'Nothing would keep her away.' Chad laughed. 'I'm pretty sure she'd have expected us to bring her ashes along if it came to that.'

'You're wicked.'

'Oh Lord, she's over in the corner with Audrey.' Chad pointed across the room. 'What're they plotting now?'

Josh shuddered. 'I dread to imagine but it probably involves all of us.'

'You're not denigrating your sweet grandmother are you?' Maggie latched onto her husband's arm.

'Nope. It's more than my life's worth.'

'Are you boys behaving?' Big J came to join them. 'You'd better not upset my favourite daughters-in-law.' He beamed and slipped an arm around Maggie and Louise's shoulders. Josh suspected his father of indulging in more than a couple of drinks from the crate of Jack Daniels he'd brought with him. 'You've got a special couple of ladies here and you'd better take good care of them or you'll have me to deal with.'

'We will.' Josh and Chad chimed their agreement together.

★　★　★

'Hey, you two lovebirds, it's time to get the speeches going.' T. Ray's booming command made Louise smile. The long distance hadn't prevented Josh's best man from travelling to Cornwall with his own new bride. 'Maggie's sister ordered me to get y'all over there.'

'I'd better find Jules because I know she wants to say a few words. Did anyone see where she went?' Louise asked.

'She's talking to my mother.' Josh pointed across the room.

Sometimes Louise forgot she had her own family these days apart from Josh and the whole Robertson clan. After getting engaged they'd visited Jules and after the initial awkwardness the two had rebuilt their relationship on a new stronger foundation. Jules had broached the touchy subject of their mother and broke the news that she'd recently discovered Cath Rogers had passed away three years earlier. It saddened them both to know she died as she'd lived most of her life, alone and struggling but made them appreciate each other even more.

Jules travelled to Nashville with her husband and three teenage children in October for a holiday and they'd enjoyed seeing all the local sights. Louise took them to see the old Robertson cabin they were renovating to become their home and the business office for The Song Sanctuary. With planning permission in place and the building well underway the music therapy centre was scheduled to open in the summer. Josh still couldn't get over the amazing support from the Nashville music community but in Louise's mind it was nothing more than her husband deserved. *Husband.* She loved that word. And him.

'Do I have something stuck in my teeth?' Josh asked.

'Pardon?'

'You're staring. I thought something must be — '

Louise wrapped her arms around his neck and kissed him. 'Everything is absolutely right and perfect. In fact I don't see how it could be any better.' Chad had persuaded Josh to use his tailor in Nashville and the charcoal-grey fine pinstripe paired with an ivory shirt and grey patterned tie perfectly set off his dark good looks. He'd warned her not to expect him to look this smart ever again but he'd willingly given her this one day. When they were on their own later she'd demonstrate her gratitude in their favourite way.

'You're damn right everything's perfect.' His hard, demanding kiss took her breath away. Josh's smile took on a dangerous hint of darkness. 'Tell me there's more lace under this,' he whispered and slid his hands over her cream lace dress.

'Oh yes. I promise.'

'When you two have quite finished could you prise your hands off each other long enough to cut a cake and listen politely to a few short speeches?' Emily playfully berated them.

'Yes, ma'am.' Josh pulled Louise along with him and they made their way to the front of the room. 'I'm guessing that cake is destined to be the go-to recipe from now on?'

Louise smiled at the gorgeous confection of almond cake layers covered with frothy white butter cream fresh raspberries and cream confection. 'As you say in the South — if it ain't broke don't fix it.' Her atrocious accent made Josh grin. 'It helped make you the groom and the best man today. My Best Man.'

'That's all I want for the rest of our lives, Mrs Joshua Robertson.'

Louise signified her agreement with a kiss that sizzled all the way down to his toes.

Thank you

Thank you for taking the time out of your busy lives to read *Here Comes the Best Man* and I hope you enjoyed it as much as I enjoyed telling Louise and Josh's story. If you could take a few moments to leave a review on a site like Amazon or on Goodreads that would be wonderful — not as an ego-boost for me — but to encourage other readers to discover my stories.

Huge thanks as always to the lovely Tasting Panel members who understood that not every hero is smooth, charming and impossibly handsome. They saw past Josh's gruff, no-nonsense exterior to the kind loyal man who would lay down his life for those he loved. If anyone deserves an HEA (happy-ever-after in romance novel terminology) it's Josh.

We do hope that you have enjoyed reading this large print book.

Did you know that all of our titles are available for purchase?

We publish a wide range of high quality large print books including:
Romances, Mysteries, Classics
General Fiction
Non Fiction and Westerns

Special interest titles available in large print are:
The Little Oxford Dictionary
Music Book, Song Book
Hymn Book, Service Book

Also available from us courtesy of Oxford University Press:
Young Readers' Dictionary
(large print edition)
Young Readers' Thesaurus
(large print edition)

For further information or a free brochure, please contact us at:
Ulverscroft Large Print Books Ltd.,
The Green, Bradgate Road, Anstey,
Leicester, LE7 7FU, England.
Tel: (00 44) **0116 236 4325**
Fax: (00 44) **0116 234 0205**

Other titles in the
Linford Romance Library:

THE LEGACY OF BLACKTHORN

June Davies

During a stormy winter's night, Meirian Penlan travels by stagecoach to take up a mysterious post at Blackthorn Manor. Wild and remote, Blackthorn lies amongst the great meres of Lancashire, surrounded by long-held superstitions, tales of witchcraft and uncanny occurrences. Once there, Meirian is drawn into a web of scandal, deception, blackmail and tragedy. Discovering old love letters and a terrible secret, she risks everything to set right a dreadful wrong — and unravel the disappearance of Blackthorn's medieval jewels . . .